It was a bogus honeymoon...

Kelly kept reminding herself as she closed her eyes and settled back into the billows of scented bubbles in the huge tub. When she opened them, she found herself looking directly at Steve.

She screamed. And ducked beneath the bubbles.

How much of her body had he seen—this man she barely knew? *Barely knew? The man was her husband!*

She couldn't hold her breath any longer and surfaced with a splash. He was still there, his face inches from hers, looking down at her.

When she heard a sound coming from the suite, she knew they were being spied on.

"Giggle," Steve whispered. "As if you were having fun."

But she was frozen. She couldn't act married!

He reached beneath the bubbles and his hand, with unerring accuracy, found her bottom and pinched it.

Then, to her absolute and total horror, he began to remove his clothes....

ABOUT THE AUTHOR

The idea for *Bride for a Night* came to Elda Minger
after a friend told her about a hilarious audition. They
laughed a lot, and later—with his permission—she
embellished his experience. Elda has empathy for both
actors and writers, having enjoyed both careers. A
gypsy at heart, she's lived throughout the United States
and Europe, and currently enjoys life in Palm Springs,
California. When she's not writing, she's usually either
gardening, dreaming, fooling around or at the movies.

Books by Elda Minger

HARLEQUIN AMERICAN ROMANCE

ELDA MINGER

BRIDE FOR A NIGHT

Harlequin Books

TORONTO • NEW YORK • LONDON
AMSTERDAM • PARIS • SYDNEY • HAMBURG
STOCKHOLM • ATHENS • TOKYO • MILAN
MADRID • WARSAW • BUDAPEST • AUCKLAND

For John, my miracle

Published January 1993

ISBN 0-373-16469-6

BRIDE FOR A NIGHT

Chapter One

Don't look down.

Kelly kept her gaze on the balcony next to hers, never taking her eyes off the railing as she contemplated the next step in her plan. Somehow it had all seemed so simple when she'd thought it up. Now, knowing she had to get from one balcony to another—nine stories up in a high-rise hotel—it felt like a plan devised by a lunatic.

Don't think. Just do it.

She didn't dare risk a glance down over Waikiki Beach. Jumping balconies hadn't really been part of her original plan when she'd decided to come to Hawaii. She'd thought that staying in the same hotel with Steve Delany, on the same floor, in the suite right next to his, that she'd have at least bumped into him by now. Then she could have slipped him her script, called it a day and jetted back home to Los Angeles and her studio apartment in the San Fernando Valley.

Nothing had gone as she'd envisioned it.

She considered the distance between the two balconies. Three feet. Three lousy feet and she was losing her nerve.

You have to get it to him.

There was nothing to do but get on with it. She'd dressed in black, deciding that she'd be less visible as she hopped from one balcony to the next. Her long, copper-colored hair had been tucked beneath a black scarf, and she wore black leather gloves. As she'd stared at herself in the full-length mirror almost half an hour ago, Kelly had thought she looked a little bit like Emma Peel.

Only Emma Peel, as smart as she was, would have never let the situation deteriorate to this level. And even if she'd had to jump balconies, she would have found some way to do it in style.

Kelly didn't even think about falling. She couldn't fall—that was that. Who would take care of Colleen if she did? Her little sister was the whole reason behind this desperate scheme, and Kelly couldn't let her down now.

The script safely tucked in the front of her ribbed, zip-front jacket, she tugged nervously at her gloves.

Here goes.

She walked to the edge of her balcony.

One good jump would have done it, but it was impossible to get up enough momentum in the small space. Kelly had decided she'd attract too much attention toting lengths of lumber through the lobby, so she'd rented a surfboard. It had seemed the only inconspicuous alternative.

They were supposed to be perfectly balanced, weren't they? she thought wildly as she carefully laid one end of the board over her balcony rail, then set the other end over Steve Delany's railing.

Can't back out now.

She'd always had a fierce concentration, and she called upon it now. Carefully balancing herself on the board, she began to inch across, knowing there would be that moment in the middle when neither balcony railing would be close at hand.

Careful, careful... Balance, balance...

Moving inch by agonizing inch, she slowly scooted across. The board was heavy and, thank God, held firm. She'd waited until the almost ever-present trade winds had settled down before attempting this, and now, at dusk, lights were beginning to twinkle up and down the length of the famous beach.

Almost there...

For some strange reason, Kelly felt like crying. It was rare she'd ever indulged herself in tears, and it was strange that her emotions should get the best of her while on a surfboard nine stories up.

There!

She was on the other side! Her hands shaking, she stood on the balcony, perfectly still and listened for any signs of activity in Steve's room.

Nothing.

She tested the sliding glass door.

Unlocked. What d' ya know.

She slid the door open, slowly, quietly, barely an inch. For one crazy instant, she was sorry she wasn't going to have to pick the lock. That had seemed like the one fun part in this entire escapade. Within seconds of that thought, she heard the sound of a shower running.

Perfect.

She could drop her script off and sneak out through the front door before Steve Delany even knew she'd been there. Hopefully he didn't travel with bodyguards the size of Stallone's, or a personal entourage like Schwarzenegger's.

Kelly eased the surfboard back on to her balcony, where it slid into place and looked as if it were simply propped up after a hard afternoon of riding the waves. Then she slid the glass door completely open on its tracks and stepped into the suite.

It looked exactly like hers—opulent and rich. Just the type of place a superstar would stay.

And superstar was exactly what Steve Delany was.

She'd researched him carefully before deciding he was the perfect candidate for her script. A major television star, Steve wanted to break into feature films. She knew he was here to audition for Dimitri Alexandros, an eccentric and volatile Greek multimillionaire. Dimitri had produced several films, most of them blockbuster vehicles that had made the actors starring in them shoot to the top.

Steve had shot to television stardom on a program called "The Nick of Time." As Nick Derringer, parttime private eye and full-time stud, he'd solved a mystery every week while living right on Waikiki Beach with his buddies. Beach living, of course, gave him plenty of opportunity to run around with his Hawaiian shirt off, exposing one of the best sets of pectoral muscles in the business.

Women loved him, men wanted to be like him. What made his show rise above the genre was the way Steve played the part. Nick was something of a devil, always breaking the fourth wall and giving the audience a cocky look while wiggling his eyebrows.

And smiling that killer smile.

No one since Burt Reynolds had been able to charm his viewers with that let's-just-have-fun look, until Nick Derringer, alias Steve Delany, appeared in living rooms across the country.

Fame had been waiting just around the corner.

Steve had caught fire with the public like gasoline ignited with a match. This massive love affair had exploded into existence almost six years ago, and showed no signs of abating. In fact, a major women's magazine had recently run a poll asking "Who would you most like to be stranded on a desert island with?"

Steve Delany had blown away the competition.

His bed was rumpled, Kelly thought absently. Stars didn't have to make their beds, did they? But then, who did, in a hotel? Expensive men's clothing—shirts and ties and slacks—was scattered over part of the bed and one of the chairs next to it. She noticed a hardback book on the coffee table and glanced curiously at the title.

Eugene O'Neill.

She was intrigued. A man, considered by most to be no more than a stud muffin, reading O'Neill? Well, why not? He'd had to have had some sort of brains to get himself into the position he was in now.

Another book caught her eye. Uta Hagen. Kelly smiled at that. So they had something in common after all, she and this Mr. Delany she'd never met. An acting teacher in New York.

Curiouser and curiouser...

A noise from the shower snapped Kelly back to the work at hand.

Get going, girl.

Where to leave the script, that was the question. On his bed? Too sexual. In the envelope or outside it? She wasn't sure. On his pillow? No, too cutesy.

The nightstand.

Perfectamento. As he switched off his light tonight, he'd notice one more thing to read.

Though I'm really no threat to O'Neill. Oh, well...

She was about to pull the script out of her jacket and put it on the nightstand when she noticed there was already a script on it. Curious, Kelly picked it up and began to skim it.

Format perfect...pacing a little slow.... Determined to read the first ten pages and see what had caught the star's eye, Kelly flipped the pages back to the very beginning.

She was on the bottom of page eight when an angry male voice broke into her thoughts.

"Who the hell are you?"

She glanced up, dropped the script to the carpeted floor and simply stared.

Steve Delany. In a towel. Muscles glistening with water. Dark hair wet and slicked off his face. Hazel eyes studying her intently.

She took all this in within the space of a heartbeat. But one impression registered above all others.

He was perturbed.

No, she thought, her writer's mind kicking in. *Angry* would be a better word.

He took a step toward her.

Perhaps *enraged,* Kelly thought as she turned and headed back the way she'd come in. Forget the front door, the balcony didn't scare her anymore.

This man did.

"Stop!"

Her feet kept moving.

"Stop, damn it!"

Move feet, move.

He tackled her, and they both slid to a heap on the carpeted floor. Kelly, who had been brought up in a tough neighborhood and had always been a tomboy at heart, wiggled and wriggled and tried desperately to get out of this man's unrelenting grip.

"Christian sent you, didn't he?" he demanded as he struggled to get her arms behind her in a vise grip.

"No, no, I don't know a Christian, I swear it! I'm not even a Christian myself, I'm a practicing Buddhist...." She knew she was babbling incoherently, but the situation called for it.

Then he lost his towel.

The knot came loose, the towel fell off. And she was on a hotel room floor with Steve Delany, and he was as naked as the day he was born.

The ladies' magazine readers would have had coronaries if they could have fantasized this. But, somehow, she was sure this particular situation wasn't at all what they'd envisioned.

She closed her eyes, deeply embarrassed.

He must have seen her embarrassment, for he loosened his grip—fractionally.

"Lady, you can't leave until I ask you a few questions. Am I making myself clear?"

"Yes," she whispered, totally mortified. She'd failed, and that knowledge weighed heavily in her heart. What now? Steve Delany would never buy a script from her after this. Thank God she hadn't even taken it out of her jacket.

"Sit still and I'll fasten my towel. Then we can...talk." He sounded as if he wanted to throw her off the balcony.

Well, Kelly decided in the split second he let go of her, *I can do that myself.*

She darted toward the sliding door.

He tackled her.

The phone rang.

They rolled around on the floor, a mass of flailing arms and legs. Kelly's fingers closed around a cord and, grasping at anything, she yanked it.

The phone fell onto the floor, the receiver fell away and an angry female voice began to speak.

"Steve? Steve? Are you there?"

Steve glanced up, startled, then glared at Kelly and put his hand over her mouth. Unfortunately, at the same time, he accidently elbowed her in the stomach.

"Owww! Get off me!" she wailed.

"Steve? Steve? What's going on?"

"Nothing, honey, I—Will you get over here and stop wiggling around?"

"Steve! Damn it, are you with *another* woman?"

"Yes, he is—I mean, no, not the way you mean!" Kelly shouted, trying desperately to rectify the situation.

"Who is she?" phone voice demanded.

"I don't know," Steve said, a placating note creeping into his voice. "Now, Pam, honey, everything's all right, and I don't want you getting upset—Will you hold still!"

"Steve!" The phone voice sounded threatening, and Kelly decided that if she still wanted to have her head attached to her shoulders this evening, it was time to make her break.

It was totally unforgivable, but it was a matter of survival. She kneed him.

"Ohhhh..." Steve let go of her and dropped to the carpeted floor, full-bodied groans coming out of his mouth. Unfortunately that same mouth was in close proximity to the phone receiver.

"Steve? Steve? What is she *doing* to you?"

"Ohhhh..."

Too late, Kelly realized her mistake. Steve's agonized groans could have easily been misconstrued for groans and moans of passion.

"Oh, my God..."

"Steve!" The string of expletives that spewed out of the receiver made Kelly wince. She stood there, hesitant, caught between Steve doubled up on the carpet and the sliding glass door—and freedom.

Common decency made her want to help him.

The will to survive told her to run like hell.

Both impulses were still warring inside her when she felt familiar fingers clamp around her ankle with deadly certainty.

He pulled her to the floor as the phone voice shrieked, "We're through!"

"YOU'VE GOTTEN ME in more trouble than any woman I've ever known. And in the shortest amount of time. That should count for something."

Kelly closed her eyes and leaned her forehead against her upraised hand. Her scarf had come off, as had her gloves and jacket. The infamous script lay on the table between them. She was starting to get a headache. Steve Delany—now dry and fully dressed— was quite understandably angry.

"I'm sorry."

"You're sorry. Great."

A tense silence passed. Kelly fidgeted, her hands moving restlessly. Forcing herself to be still, she stared at her hands, now in her lap, as if they were the most fascinating appendages on earth.

"I really am."

"So am I. You have no idea what this little stunt of yours cost me."

She swallowed against the abject misery clogging her throat. "Did you love her?"

"Did I love who?"

"The woman on the phone."

"No."

"Oh."

Another tense silence ensued, then Steve picked up her script and began to thumb through it.

"So that's what this was all about, huh? Getting me to read your script."

"Yeah." She couldn't meet his eyes. If it were possible to feel lower than an earthworm, then this was exactly how that felt. How could she have thought this plan had a chance of working?

"I can't believe how you've totally screwed things up."

She didn't get it, and decided at that moment she had absolutely nothing to lose by trying to understand.

"How? I mean, if you didn't love Pam, you didn't lose much of anything, right?"

"That isn't all there was to it."

"Well, if you tell me, maybe... I can help you."

"Your kind of help I don't need."

Kelly felt a wild desperation building inside her. She wasn't a vindictive person by nature, and abhorred meanness in others. Now, knowing she'd hurt this innocent man, she had to get to the bottom of it.

"No, I really mean it. I wish there was some way I could fix things." When he didn't answer, she blurted out, "At least let me know what I've done!"

"Sure. Why not?" Steve slumped back in his chair, threw the script onto the table and ran a frustrated hand through his thick, dark hair. "This is it, in a nutshell. I was supposed to meet Dimitri Alexandros for drinks tonight, and Pam was supposed to come with me. Dimi's really big on the whole family thing, so I thought if I made it sound as if I were engaged, I'd have a better chance at getting the part. Got it?"

She wrinkled up her nose as she stared at him, thinking.

"Wait. Were you guys really engaged?"

"Sort of."

"What's that mean?"

"It means that it was a means to an end for me and that Pammie was really starting to get into it."

"Like how?" Kelly's writer's instincts and curiosity were starting to take over. Her woman's empathy sensed that Steve needed to talk about it.

"Getting a little bossy. Starting to drop hints to the press. We weren't really supposed to be engaged, but she was going nuts if I even looked at another woman." He sighed, then looked down at the script on the table. "She was getting to be a real pain in the butt, but I can't help wishing our engagement had lasted through the night."

"Surely Dimi would still hire you even if you are a bachelor. I mean, you're a wonderful actor." That just sort of slipped out, and Kelly felt herself coloring. What a goofball fan-type thing to say.

"You think so? Thanks." He hesitated. "You liked the show?"

Actors. "Caught it every week. You had some good writers on staff."

"Can't survive without 'em." He flashed a grin so like Nick Derringer's that it almost took her breath away. There was a totally surreal quality to this entire conversation. It was like being a guest star on "The Nick of Time," only, the entire scene was being improvised. Kelly couldn't help but smile as she thought of Nick Derringer telling her, "Don't worry, ma'am, we'll find a way to get him back."

She caught his eye on her, studying her.

"What?" She touched her hair. "What?"

"A surfboard. You climbed over on a surfboard." He shook his head, then riffled the pages of her script. "Lady, you're truly nuts. Gutsy, but nuts."

He didn't seem mad anymore. She thought of asking him to take a look at her script, then decided not to push her luck.

"I'd better get going. I've got to get packed. I'm checking out tomorrow."

He gestured toward the wall that divided the two suites. "That's why you're here? Because of me?"

"Yeah."

"It's an expensive hotel."

"Tell me about it."

"Is it a good script?"

Her heart lodged in her mouth. She swallowed. *Oh, God.* "Yes," she whispered.

"Agented?"

She nodded her head.

"I'll take a look at it," he said.

"Oh, God, oh, Mr. Delany—"

"I figure, you risk your life, you deserve something."

"Thank you, thank you, thank you—"

"I'm not promising anything, but…remember you said you wished there was a way you could fix things?"

"Yeah."

"Well, I thought of something. I think we can make a deal."

Oh, no. She still felt guilty about the way she'd messed up Steve's chance at the big time. But the look in his hazel eyes made her suddenly uneasy. This man was used to getting what he wanted in any negotiation.

"You really could help me out."

She was getting glimpses of that famous Delany charm, that quality that had helped him become a television star. And her instincts were screaming at her to go slowly, carefully, to not allow herself to be bowled over by his appeal.

"Well, I meant within reason, of course."

"It's nothing that hard. Just come with me for drinks tonight, so Dimi can see you. Pretend we're on the verge of getting engaged, and convince him I'm really a stable, family-type guy."

"I couldn't do that!"

"Why not?"

"It would be lying."

"Think of it as acting. This drink with Dimi tonight is as much of an audition as if he asked me to come to a studio."

She was seeing the cleverness and intelligence that had made Steve Delany a household name. And she had a feeling that he wasn't going to take no for an answer.

But she still had to resist.

"He'll never buy it."

"He will. People see what they want to see."

She hesitated, trying to think of another argument. But Steve moved in, with all the intensity and drive that had gotten him well on his way to the top.

"If you hadn't messed things up in the first place—"

"Fine. One night, one drink, that's it." Something about this man made her want to set limits. She didn't want to lose control of the situation.

"That's all it'll take. And I'll make sure your script gets to some major people at the studios."

Somehow she knew he'd keep his promise.

"So, Kelly, do we have a deal?" He held out his hand and looked her directly in the eye.

She raised her hand and he shook it firmly.

"Yeah. We do. I mean, one night and one little drink. What harm can there be in that?"

"Great. I'll pick you up at eleven-thirty. We're supposed to meet him at midnight."

"Deal. What should I wear?"

"Hmmm. What've you got?"

Within minutes, they were both in her suite, staring at her meager wardrobe in dismay.

"I'm sorry, Mr. Delany."

"Steve, it's Steve. If you're my fiancée, this Mr. Delany business won't cut it." He glanced around the suite impatiently, as if he could find the answer in one of the room's corners. "This is getting complicated."

"I have some money left. I could go buy a dress."

"Money's not the issue. Time is." He snapped his fingers. "Luis!"

"Luis?"

"He owes me."

She didn't know what he was talking about, but just watched as he picked up her phone and began to punch out a number. She stood by the bed, wondering what was going to happen next.

"Luis? Steve. I'm in a jam and I need your help. Look, I know you're already closed, but could I send you someone? By tonight. Yeah. Yeah. It's an emergency." He eyed her with a speculative gaze, then said, "I think we're talking major makeover here—"

"Hey!"

"Great. She'll be there in twenty minutes." He hung up the phone and turned toward her. "Come on, I'll give you money for a cab. Luis is a friend of mine from the show. He's going to open his shop and make you over. Just be back by eleven-thirty sharp."

Everything was happening so fast, Kelly didn't have time to protest. She grabbed her purse and followed Steve out the suite to the bank of elevators. As they stepped inside one, Kelly said, "What was this about a major makeover?"

The door slid shut.

"DARLING, YOUR HAIR! When did you last have a trim?"

Luis was in his late thirties, with thick, shiny black hair pulled back in a ponytail. Slender, quick, graceful, dressed in a bright red jumpsuit, he hovered around Kelly like an enormous, colorful hummingbird. Abrupt, truthful and outrageous, he had a way of getting straight to the point.

She liked him immediately.

"Six, eight months ago."

"*Quelle horreur!* What did they use? A weed whacker?" He picked up his scissors and Kelly closed her eyes, tensed and bit her lip.

"Not short. I hate short hair."

"Not short, darling. But we need to put a little order into this mane."

She could hear the scissors snipping, and she thought of the scene in *The Wizard of Oz* when the Cowardly Lion had his hair done and his nails painted. All right, maybe the shopping trip montage and makeover in *Pretty Woman*. Whatever, the evening was turning into a revelation.

She'd never had too much time to think about pampering herself. There were always bills to pay, collection agencies to mollify, landladies to pacify, disasters to avert. It seemed she'd been running from the time her mother died to the moment she'd set her butt down in this chair.

"Beautiful color, darling. My customers would kill for this coppery shade."

"Thanks," she replied, her voice tense.

"Open your eyes, *mon ange!* Luis will not disappoint you!"

She chanced a peek. Wet, her hair lay around her shoulders and down her back in a dark, wavy mass. Luis had already washed and conditioned it, and now he was snipping away—only about three inches.

"Too much damage." Luis sniffed. "Six months— six years is more like it."

She smiled. "I can't remember the last time I had a haircut."

Luis laughed, his delight evident. "Good. Be honest with me so I can fix you."

"Major makeover, huh?"

He laughed again. "You heard? And it made you mad, *non?*"

"Yeah."

"Not so major, I think. Just a little—how do you say?"

"Neglect?"

"Neglect. But not anymore."

IT WAS LIKE STARING at a stranger.

Luis had released the natural wave in her hair, and it was wild and free, cut to just below her shoulders. The facial had taken care of her dry skin, and skillful makeup had done the rest. The manicure and pedicure had been fun, as had the upper-body mud mask.

But the clothes were inspired.

Luis's shop was a woman's paradise, the salon on one side, the boutique on the other. Blithely informing her that Steve would pick up the tab, Luis had selected a shimmering slip of a dress, constructed almost entirely of sequins.

"Too dressy?" Kelly had asked.

"Not for Dimi—he likes flash. The question is, do you?"

"I don't know."

"I think you do. You must walk in like you own the place, yes?"

She nodded her head.

The dress. Wonderful, wispy, high-heeled evening shoes. Opera-length gloves.

"Oh, no!"

"Oh, yes!" Luis replied. "They are so wicked. Dimi likes wicked women, flirtatious women, dangerous women. He will be—delighted."

"You're sure?"

"But of course."

She hesitated, then touched one of the gloves. "Do I drink with these things on?"

"No. They are—how do you say—?"

"Accessories?"

"Ah, yes. You go to the table. You pout prettily. You look at Steve with the hunger in your eyes. Then, when the drinks are served, you slowly take one glove off and put it on the table. It will get him thinking those thoughts—you know what I mean?"

She wasn't sure she wanted Steve Delany thinking those particular thoughts about her. This little escapade tonight was strictly business, then she was jetting back to Los Angeles.

"Luis, you're sure?"

"*Absolument.* We are usually casual on the islands, but Dimi is taking you to his private club, The White Orchid. You must stand out. Get his attention and help Steve."

"You know?"

"I knew about that Pam." He sniffed elegantly, his opinion of the woman perfectly clear. "And I see you, and I say . . . this could get *very* interesting."

Kelly smiled. She'd been lonely in Hawaii the past few days while she'd tracked Steve. It felt so good to simply talk to someone. Especially Luis, whom she instinctively felt had her best interests at heart.

"Now, quickly, *mon ange.* Earrings, no necklace. The dress does not call for it. And perfume, wonderful perfume that will have both men at your feet. . . ."

STEVE LOCKED THE DOOR of his suite after him, then pocketed the key. He was worried about the evening, but not about Kelly. If anyone could work miracles, it was Luis.

It wasn't that Kelly was a bad-looking woman. She just didn't have that cared-for look that most of the women he dated possessed. Luis would polish her up, make her shine.

She was kind of cute, in a girl-next-door kind of way. Like someone's little sister, with her long hair pulled back in a ponytail and her upturned nose. Her skin had that fresh-scrubbed look, her eyes were blindingly honest. There had been something so…guileless about her. Something that had touched him. Maybe that's why he'd agreed to read her blasted script.

He chuckled as he thought of her climbing over onto his balcony on a surfboard. *Crazy Kelly…* Well, if she had the nerve to do that, tonight should be a piece of cake.

Steve adjusted his jacket, smoothed the lapels. Taking a deep breath, he rapped a sharp greeting on Kelly's door.

"Coming." Her voice sounded far away, inside the suite.

On time. How nice.

Then Kelly opened the door and knocked his socks off.

The impact she made on his senses made his knees weak. He had a quick impression of a mane of coppery-colored hair, sultry green eyes, a beautiful mouth and a drop-dead sequined dress encasing a rather

drop-dead little body. Endless legs, beautiful legs—
how had he missed those *legs?*

Steve Delany, famous actor and master cynic, took
one long look at Kelly Archer and promptly fell head
over heels in lust.

Chapter Two

It promised to be the easiest acting job he'd ever done in his life.

What had happened to the girl next door? Steve thought as he and Kelly sat in the back seat of the limousine Dimitri had sent for them. In the blink of an eye—well, closer to almost five hours—she'd been transformed into Jessica Rabbit.

I'm not bad... I'm just drawn that way.

He couldn't believe the metamorphosis. Luis had truly outdone himself.

Steve had always considered himself a man who could size up a person instantly. While he'd been furious with Kelly earlier in his room, had wrestled on the floor with her, been tempted to pin her down and had finally sat directly across the table from her beneath a bright light, the one thing he'd been sure of was that he wasn't attracted to her.

Until now.

Talk about a major wrench. He'd thought she'd thrown the ultimate one earlier this evening, but it was nothing compared to the complications these feelings brought into his master plan. One of the reasons he'd suggested she pose as his fiancée was that there was absolutely no potential for the kinds of complications that Pam had brought to the deal.

Steve frowned, then tore his gaze away from Kelly and looked out the limousine's window. He didn't like feeling out of control, it wasn't a situation that he encouraged—ever.

Get the part. Forget the girl.

He smiled, thinking of what Nick Derringer would do.

Get the part. Nail the girl. Solve the case.

But he wasn't Nick, he was an actor who badly wanted a part in Dimitri Alexandros's next film.

Forget the girl.

Wise, cold, calculating advice. He wasn't really that cold a man, but this was his big break and he was smart enough to know it. Being an actor, a gypsy who roamed all over the world in search of great parts and a chance to express himself through them, he'd given considerable thought to relationships. Promising more than he could deliver had never seemed fair to the women involved, because he could truly, honestly, promise them absolutely nothing. Zip.

He'd never wanted to commit until he'd given himself every chance to find his niche in life. And, since he'd turned eighteen, he'd been positive that acting was it.

No promises, no ties, nothing. He'd been too busy to feel lonely, too driven to care.

Until Jessica came along. . . .

She smelled incredible, a soft, sultry scent. The little number she was wearing exposed an amazing amount of skin. She wasn't tanned, so the deep blue, glittery material was the perfect foil to her pale skin and blazing hair. Luis had pulled part of it away from her face with a glittery comb, to which he had attached one perfect, white orchid.

Clever.

Steve was surprised by how strong the urge was to pull it out of her hair, run his fingers through the silken waves and ease her down on the back seat of the limo. He'd really liked the love scene in *No Way Out*, and his imagination went into overdrive at the thought of running his hands up Kelly's legs....

Another part of his anatomy, distinctly male, went into overdrive at the exact same moment his imagination did.

He had to force himself to remember why they were attempting to pull off this charade in the first place.

The part.

The limo was slowing down as it made the turn into the nightclub's parking lot. Steve turned toward Kelly, and was as astonished as she was by the words that popped out of his mouth.

"Kiss me."

"I BEG YOUR PARDON?" she replied softly. It had to be the gloves. He'd been looking at her strangely since he'd picked her up.

"Kiss me."

"Here?"

"No, out on the hood. Of course, here!"

"Why?"

He seemed to be thinking on his feet, and she sensed he was searching for a reason. She wondered if he was gifted at improvisation or needed a script.

"Because Dimi's a sly old fox, and he'll know something's up if we're not comfortable with each other. If I muss you up a little, it'll look like we can't take our hands off each other. He'll love it."

There was a short, pregnant pause as Kelly digested this.

"You think so?"

He nodded his head.

"Okay. But no tongues."

"Kelly—"

"We only met this evening, and I don't think I'd be comfortable with that."

He was silent.

She was so uncomfortable that she blurted out the first thing she thought.

"Do you like my hair this way?"

"Do you always say the first thing that comes to your mind?"

"Most of the time."

He sighed. "C'mere."

He kissed her, a soft, gentle kiss, full on the lips. Very pleasant . . . more than pleasant. She was horrified at the little thrill of pleasure that rippled up and down her spine.

This is not smart.

"Let's go." He was already getting out of the limousine and she followed him, the ocean wind blowing her hair around her face, her high heels tapping briskly against the cement.

"How long does Dimi think we've known each other?"

"Three weeks."

"Three weeks!" She had to walk fast to keep up with him. Now that they were there, he seemed impatient for the evening to begin.

"I'm a fast worker." He flashed her that killer grin, and she was shocked to find herself wondering how he looked in the morning. In bed.

Too good, I'll bet.

"Do we know each other's families?"

"No."

"Was I vacationing here?"

"You got it."

"Any quirks I should know about?"

"Yours or mine?"

"Mine."

"Nah, play it by ear. Dimi doesn't know anything about Pam. We'll have to improvise."

She hated the color that heated her cheeks at the next thought, but she had to ask it.

"Have we slept together?"

"You bet." He wiggled his eyebrows.

She punched his arm and he grabbed her hand as they entered The White Orchid.

It screamed of money, *lots* of money, but in a casual, laid-back way that had probably been influenced by the islands. Kelly had a quick impression of soft lighting, brilliant tropical flowers, peach tablecloths and envious feminine glances as they wended their way through the dining area toward a large table with an ocean view.

Dimitri Alexandros was sitting by himself, a glass of red wine in front of him. He rose from his seat as they approached, and Kelly was struck by the raw, earthy sense of power that emanated from this man. His hair was thick and completely silver, his tanned face creased and lined with experience. The suit was expensive. The diamond set in the ring on his finger was probably worth the combined assets of several small South American countries.

But it was his eyes, dark, inquisitive and so very alive, that drew her to him instantly.

"Hello," she said, her delight registering in her voice. The pictures she'd seen in the paper in no way did this man justice.

"Ah, so this is the one," Dimitri said to Steve as he visually assessed her. "Very nice."

"Thank you," she murmured.

"I think," said Steve, "that compliment was meant for me."

She smiled up at him, determined to play this part to the hilt and make sure he got the role. "But I think I got a good deal, too."

Dimitri laughed.

Introductions were quickly made, then he motioned for them to join him. "I'd forgotten how outspoken American women are, Kelly." He smiled at her, his eyes warm. "A quality I adore."

Kelly felt Steve tense beside her as Dimitri reached for her hand, lifted and kissed it. "Now, sit. We have much to discuss."

She thought they were going to plunge into a discussion about Dimitri's movie right away, and was surprised when he asked, "So, how did you meet this ruffian?"

She thought wildly, wishing Steve had given her more clues. "On the beach. I was—surfing."

Dimitri didn't say anything for a few seconds, and Kelly rushed to fill the silence. "It was—late in the evening. Just about sunset. I could tell he was just as surprised as I was by the—explosiveness of that first meeting. We made—an unforgettable impression on each other—"

Steve kicked her gently under the table, and she closed her mouth, then smiled across the table at the millionaire.

Dimitri's expression reflected his puzzlement as he turned toward Steve. "I thought you said you met her by the pool."

Before Steve could reply, Kelly kicked him back. *Improvise, indeed.* "Well, actually, we first saw each other on the beach, but actually talked by the hotel pool."

"Ahh."

Their waiter, hovering and respectful, prepared to take their order.

"Just a Coke for me," Steve said.

"I'll have one of those big fruit drinks with the little umbrellas," Kelly said.

"You drink?" Dimitri asked.

"I don't? I mean, I don't. I just started today." She knew she was babbling, and was astonished when Steve's hand came down over one of hers, stilling its restless movement. His touch calmed her, and she smiled at Dimitri, determined to set the matter straight.

"I just thought . . . every girl should have a hobby, don't you think?"

"Of course."

They chatted pleasantly, their drinks arrived and Dimitri acted as if they were seated in his private living room. Kelly felt comfortable in his presence, but she didn't let down her guard. Dimitri Alexandros hadn't become a multimillionaire by acting like Santa Claus.

"So, Kelly, why do you think I should give your fiancé a part in my newest film?"

The question floored her. She'd thought all she was going to have to do this evening was play the part of the accessory, the little woman to Steve's big man. Kelly didn't even know what the screenplay was about. Steve hadn't thought to tell her that, either.

Of course his fiancée would have known.

"Hmmm," she said, stalling for time. She could feel Steve tensing beside her, and her heart ached for him. Being a writer, in a similar sort of career, she knew this was a big, big break for him, and her empathy was boundless.

"I'm warning you in advance," she said softly, leaning toward Dimitri, "I'm going to be prejudiced."

Dimitri laughed, clearly delighted. "An honest woman. How rare in this world."

Kelly thought desperately. She had to get some clues, remember . . .

Then it clicked into place. She'd read it in the trades two weeks ago, when she'd been researching Steve. An action-adventure film, with a strong romantic sub-plot. Steve was up for the hero, a character similar to Jack Colter in *Romancing the Stone*.

"Well, you know from his work on "The Nick of Time" that he can carry both a romantic lead and an action-adventure type of plot."

Dimitri nodded his head, his attention never leaving her.

"And he was just voted the man most women wanted to be stranded on a desert island with. But I knew that."

The older man's lips were starting to twitch.

"Women love him. In fact, there was a woman today who was extremely angry because we were together—"

Steve's hand, covering hers, squeezed gently as if to say, *Don't get carried away.*

"I understand what you mean, Kelly. He engenders the most extraordinary loyalty in his fans."

"Because he gives them what they want. A hero they can believe in, look up to, fantasize about. A man they can love." She looked over at Steve. Though his expression was perfectly impassive, she could see the surprise in the depths of his hazel eyes.

She found she liked surprising him.

"Anything else I should know about?" Dimitri asked.

"Just that he's a hard worker, he won't hold up your production or waste your money and he wants this part very badly. It's the right time for him, and this part is the right part." Instinct told her to lay all her cards on the table with this man. It would be impossible to pull the wool over his eyes.

Except, of course, for the phony fiancée bit.

Dimitri was quiet for such a long moment that Kelly feared she'd blown it. Then he glanced from her face to Steve's.

"You're a lucky man, to inspire such love and loyalty."

"I know I am," Steve replied quietly. He slid his hand down her arm, his fingers caressing her skin, and she felt herself come alive at his touch. A blush rose in her face and she glanced down at the linen tablecloth. When she finally met Dimitri's gaze, he was smiling at her.

"To you, marriage is forever, is it not?"

"Yes," she whispered.

"And I know this—you're a romantic."

Boy, was that the truth. "Yes."

He turned his attention to Steve. "You must marry this girl."

She felt Steve's arm come around her, in a sort of wordless agreement.

"It's yours, then, Steve. I give it to you."

For just an instant, Kelly couldn't believe her ears. He got the part. Just like that. She didn't realize how happy she'd be to know she made up for all the damage she'd done earlier in the evening.

They talked for almost an hour longer, about movies they'd seen, actor's performances they'd admired, the state of the industry, Greece and Dimi's fabulous yacht, *The Aphrodite.*

Dimitri was delighted to learn that Kelly had been to Greece.

"Just Athens. And we took a day trip to the Oracle at Delphi. My mother had always wanted to go, so she found a way."

"And you liked it?"

"I just loved it. Greece is the most beautiful country. I've always wanted to go back, especially to the islands."

"You must come to my island one day."

"I'd like that."

"It is a most romantic country. You've never been to Greece, Steve?"

"Never."

"Hmmm." Dimitri studied them both for a moment, then smiled. "A situation that should be rectified as soon as possible."

"Perhaps after filming," Steve suggested. "A quiet honeymoon."

"Honey," Kelly said, touching Steve's arm. "I think I'm going to go back to our room. I'm getting a little tired and I know you and Mr. Alexandros have a lot more to talk about." She needed to get away from Steve. She didn't like the direction her thoughts and emotions were taking her. A honeymoon in Greece...

A honeymoon with Nick Derringer. The two of them in bathing suits, lying by the pounding surf, his muscles oiled and glistening, the sunlight reflecting off that body....

The sunlight making your head soft! Get your thoughts out of the clouds and back to the deal.

"I'd really better leave the two of you so you can discuss business," she murmured.

"Let me call Marco. He can drive you," said Dimitri.

As he signaled for a phone to be brought to their table, Kelly studied the man. You wouldn't want to cross him in anything, for Dimitri was both powerful and stubborn. Used to having his own way. One thing Kelly knew with certainty was that Dimitri Alexandros would make a formidable enemy.

Or a lifelong, loyal friend.

They chatted a few minutes longer, then Marco appeared silently, standing by the table and awaiting Dimitri's command.

"It was enchanting to meet you, Miss Archer."

"Thank you, Dimitri. I enjoyed meeting you."

"You must come to my country—I'll see to it."

"I'd like that."

Steve stood up as she did, and she was surprised when he gently pulled her into his arms and kissed her.

The same little thrill coursed through her. Chemistry didn't understand phony engagements, and as Steve kissed her, a part of Kelly's mind registered that there was something very powerful going on between them.

Of course, considering he was Steve Delany, alias Nick Derringer, he had something powerful going on with the greater part of America's female population. Maybe this was nothing new to Steve. Maybe she should just relax and enjoy it.

Maybe, she thought, shocking herself, *you're getting a little jealous.*

Remembering the infamous Pam, Kelly determined to play it cool. But she would give Dimitri a little something that would seal their charade.

"Don't be too long, darling," she whispered, stroking Steve's cheekbone with her gloved hand. She'd been so nervous, she'd forgotten to take them off, but considering how the evening had progressed, it couldn't be considered a deadly faux pas.

"Wait up for me," he said, the tiniest glint of humor in his eyes.

She smiled back, happy for him. Steve Delany was most definitely on his way.

SUCH A DEAL . . .

Back in her hotel suite, Kelly finished packing. It was almost four in the morning before she was done, and she went out onto her balcony and looked out over the beach. As far up as she was, she could still hear the sound of waves crashing against the shore. The wind caressed her skin, perfumed with the essence of tropical flowers.

A part of her, that part that relished traveling and creating new experiences for herself, wished she'd had a chance to see more of this island. She'd always wanted to come to Hawaii, but had never thought the decision would be made at the last minute, and out of complete desperation.

Her eleven-year-old sister, Colleen, needed delicate heart surgery, and theirs had never been a family rolling in dough. With very few options, Kelly's plan had been born. She'd spent most of her life walking a tightrope without any safety net, and had seen absolutely no reason to start playing it safe when her sister's life was at stake.

Their Aunt Bette had taken both girls in when their mother had died, and Kelly had silently vowed never to be a burden to the aunt she adored. Bette had a reputation as the bad girl of the family, because she liked flashy clothes, smoked clove cigarettes and had a number of what their grandmother had called "gentleman callers."

Kelly had adored her, and still did.

What they'd lacked in money, they'd made up for in love and laughter. Living in an old beachfront house in Florida, the three of them had been content to meet each day as it came. Bette had encouraged her niece's dreams, treating them as seriously as any other aspect of their lives.

And Kelly had started dreaming big.

She'd always read, spent all her allowance on books. Her library card had been well-worn by the time she was eight. Books had been her outlet for her hunger of adventure. In a book, she could do or be anything she wanted, there were no limits.

Then, that one morning around the kitchen table, Colleen had suggested she write one.

Lying now on the bed, thinking of her baby sister, Kelly smiled. What Colleen lacked in physical robustness, she'd made up for in spirit. From the moment Kelly had held her sister in her arms at the hospital, she'd known Colleen was special.

She made everyone feel loved.

Bette might have been the colorful dreamer of their little household, and Kelly might have been its fighting spirit, but Colleen had given their home its heart. It was nothing Kelly could put into words, but Colleen had always made her feel loved.

"Write a book?" she'd said. "About what?"

"You'll find something wonderful," Colleen had said.

The amazing thing was, she'd been only six at the time.

When Bette had suggested they move to Los Angeles, Colleen had jumped up and down with excitement. There were professional writers in Hollywood, weren't there? Kelly could learn everything she needed to know and make the necessary connections, couldn't she?

They'd made the drive in five days, everything the three of them owned crammed into their old Chevy station wagon, and had set up housekeeping in Hollywood. The city reminded Kelly of Florida, with its palm trees and abundant vegetation. But the air was drier, like a desert being held at bay. Kelly fell in love with the city, with its lush, green, overgrown hills, its lurid neon signs and the strange assortment of people populating its streets.

It was a shabby little town, but it had a magical, special feel. Anything could happen. Rags to riches. Fame and fortune. Kelly had been determined to make enough money so her little family would always be safe.

Their work began. While Colleen went to grade school, Kelly found a job waitressing. Every spare moment, every spare dime, went into classes. Then she took a class in screenwriting, and fell head over heels. Hard. Forever.

They'd always watched movies, thrilled over Scarlett's exploits, cried over *Casablanca*, laughed at the Marx Brothers. But Kelly had never thought of screenwriting as practical. If writing and publishing a novel had seemed like a long shot, selling a screenplay promised to be a trip to the moon.

Colleen's faith had been unshakable over the years.

"You can do it, Kelly," she'd say. "One page a day is a first draft in four months. You just have to have a little faith."

Faith. Her sister had more than her share. Colleen had become sick again shortly after their move, and they'd had to take her out of school. Her heart, the doctor had said. Surgery. With a topflight doctor, she'd have a chance at a normal life.

A chance.

By this time, Kelly had sold some short screenplays to cable for modest amounts of money. She had an agent. Now she had to start thinking in terms of big bucks for big medical bills. Over countless cups of coffee at their kitchen table, she and Bette had launched their plan.

They'd scrimped and saved for Kelly's airfare to Hawaii—the cheapest ticket possible. They'd budgeted in one night for her at an expensive hotel. And Kelly had sat down, with absolutely no fear in her heart, and written the screenplay of her career.

Which was now in Steve Delany's hands.

Well, she'd done what she'd set out to do. Steve had the part and that had to have made him happy. She couldn't expect him to read her screenplay before her plane left tomorrow afternoon. That was really asking too much.

But perhaps . . . if he knew . . . if she told him about her little sister, and what the money would mean to her . . .

She was so deep in thought that the brisk knock on her door made her start upright.

"Steve?" she called out.

"It's me," he answered.

She pulled on her bathrobe, tied the belt tightly, then opened the door. He swept into the room, throwing his jacket onto the sofa. His glance took in the pristine order of her suite, the packed suitcase, tomorrow's clothing laid out on a chair and finally the glittering dress hanging forlornly in the front closet.

"You're leaving?"

She sighed. "I have to get home. Family responsibilities and all that."

He stared at her intently. "You're married?"

"Oh, no. I mean, my aunt and my sister."

"Kelly, listen. I can't thank you enough—"

She couldn't bear this goodbye. "It's okay. I mean, I messed it up and it's only right that I should fix it. It wouldn't have been right for me to have waltzed out and left you in the lurch—" To her horror, her emotions were skating perilously close to the surface. She couldn't bear the thought of going home and telling Colleen she'd have to wait just a little longer. . . .

"Kelly?" He was looking at her, concern in his eyes.

"It's okay. I—I'm just tired and I have a long day ahead tomorrow and I have to get back and make sure that everything's—"

"Want to tell me about it?"

"Not really."

"You're sure? Sometimes it just helps to talk."

"Not this time."

They faced each other, sitting on the sofa, for what seemed like an endless amount of time—though it couldn't have been more than a minute.

"Then, can I say something?" Steve asked.

Kelly found a tissue in her bathrobe pocket and blew her nose. "Sure."

"I think we should get married."

Chapter Three

"*What?*"

"I think we should get married."

"What happened to one drink and one night?"

"Things have . . . changed."

"Get married? The two of us?"

"No, you and Dimitri. Of course you and me."

He couldn't be serious. She stared up at him, trying to imagine what could have given him such a crazy idea.

Dimitri.

"Is it your part? He won't give you the part unless we're married?"

"No, it's not that . . . simple."

"What is it, then?"

"Well, you kind of did too good a job. Dimi fell head over heels for the idea of the two of us getting married. He feels as if he 'knows your spirit'—that's what he said, exactly. He doesn't want a romantic like you to wait any longer than necessary to have a happy home life."

"He told you all this?" It was a lot to have thrown at her all at once, and she needed a moment to adjust to the idea. Married to Steve? She didn't like the way her traitorous thoughts were taking her.

This idea sounded just a little too good.

"You'd *marry* me to keep a part in this film?"

Steve actually looked flustered, and she was delighted to know this was possible. She'd always mistrusted people who had no feelings.

"It wouldn't be an actual marriage. It wouldn't even have to be consummated. It would be like one of those marriages—"

"—A marriage of convenience. A classic plot device."

"Yeah. One of those."

"What happens after the movie's finished?"

"We get a divorce."

"A *divorce* of convenience? And stay friends? After something like that?"

He started to laugh. "Yeah. We could stay friends."

"I think you're nuts." She studied him for a long moment, wrinkling her nose while she thought. "It doesn't make sense. Couldn't we just keep him thinking we're engaged? Anyway, I have to get home and—"

"No way. Dimi has to be kept thinking I'm a happily involved man. There are . . . a couple of reasons that I just found out."

"Like?"

"You're acting like a wife already. Couldn't we just go ahead with this because I think it's a good idea?"

"No."

He sighed. "Okay."

She could sense his nervousness as he raked his fingers through his hair. They were still sitting on the sofa, but a little more relaxed now.

"It's like this. Dimi is giving his mistress the lead female role in this movie, and until he found out I was involved with you tonight, I was totally out of the running."

"But why?"

He was silent for too long.

She trusted what her instincts were screaming at her.

"You were *involved* with her?"

He nodded.

"Big affair?"

"No. One weekend. But she kind of blew it up out of proportion when she told Dimi."

"She *told* him?"

"Donnatella's like no other woman I've ever met."

Donnatella Marciano. Temperamental. Italian. Jealous. Passionate. Wild and sultry and guaranteed to raise men's blood pressure—among other things—when she appeared on the big screen.

"Let me get this straight. You had an affair with Donnatella Marciano, and Dimi actually believes you'd go from that sex goddess to me?"

She watched, fascinated, as a muscle in his cheek jumped. His jawline was taut, his expression controlled, and she had a feeling that this was a man who normally didn't like to kiss and tell. Only the fact that she'd demanded to know everything had wrung this little confession out of him.

"It's not so hard to understand. Donnatella's charms fade pretty quickly when you aren't between the sheets with her. Dimi has enough money to keep her amused and out of his hair.''

''Did you—did you love her?''

''What is this with you and love? We did a picture together, in Italy, in a little village that didn't even have a movie theater. We both got bored—'' He stopped, apparently registering the look on her face. ''Look, I'm not saying what I did was right, but she knew the score going in. We both had a good time and we moved on, only she told Dimi and he's a little nervous about having me around Donnatella if I'm not on a suitable leash.''

''That's what marriage is to you? A leash?''

''No, that's not what I meant. Dimi's nervous. He thinks Donnatella may want to start things up with me again.''

''Do you?''

''Not in this lifetime.''

''Good. But if you don't want to start up with her, what's Dimi worried about?''

''He thinks he's getting too old for her, so he never lets Donnatella socialize with men who are younger than he is. Unless you're around as a kind of…safety valve, I could lose the part before filming starts.''

She considered her options, and knew that this arrangement was too emotionally frightening to contemplate.

''I have to get back. I have business at home.''

''I'll help you take care of it.''

''I have to go to some studio meetings in Los Angeles.'' *An utter lie, of course, but all's fair…*

"If you're married to me, they'll let you take them over the phone."

She caught the necessary arrogance, just enough, that had made him a star.

"I have family obligations I can't put off."

"I'll help you take care of them."

She paused, thinking furiously. Then Steve dropped the bomb.

"Besides, if you marry me, I can guarantee you a lot of money within a few days."

This caught her full attention immediately. "How?"

"We get married, we arrange to sell the pictures to one of those tabloid papers, you pocket the change. Whatever you need the money for, it's yours."

The image of wiring Aunt Bette the money made her go absolutely still.

"Hey, c'mon, if it's that bad an idea—"

"No, no, it's not that." Her voice was very calm, as if another person were saying the words. "It's nothing like that at all."

"What?"

"It's my little sister. She's really ill, we don't have any money, and she needs this operation—"

The words poured out of her, it was such a relief to tell someone, to share it with someone for a change. She hadn't wanted to tell him, but if they were going to be together for any length of time, she would have had to. It wasn't the sort of secret she could have kept for long.

He was silent for almost a minute. She glanced up at him. Steve had the strangest expression on his face, as if he were in physical pain. When he finally spoke, his voice was rough.

"That's the worst there is, to know someone you love needs you, and be unable to help."

"I know you think I'm a nutcase—"

"No." He moved closer to her on the sofa, then covered one of her hands with his. "No, I don't. I would have done the same thing."

"Okay, so if we do this, what's our next move?"

"I give you a ring, we let Dimi give us a wedding, we sell the pictures, your sister gets her surgery, I do the part and everybody's happy."

"And we stay friends?"

"Yeah."

"It can't be that simple."

"Yes it can."

"One drink, one night, now one marriage and eventually one divorce. Any more surprises for me?"

"None. As soon as it's over, the deal's done."

"Promise?"

"Promise."

"And no fooling around?"

"You have my word." But his mouth quirked up at the corners, and she couldn't help smiling back. Damn the man. His charm was a lethal weapon.

"What's so funny?"

"You. You're different from any woman I've ever met."

"Because I don't want to—consummate things?"

"That, and a few other things."

"I guess I'm just not in sync with American womanhood. A jug of wine, a desert island and thou—"

"Not a lot of fun, when you get passed over for parts."

That she understood, the frustration of a creative career.

"I'm sorry. Okay. Another deal. One marriage, but we don't live together, we don't fool around and we quietly get divorced after you bag the part."

"You got it. You'll do it?"

"Okay. But if there's any trouble, we talk it out?"

"Sure."

"We can be honest with each other?"

"Yeah. It'll be simple."

IT'LL BE SIMPLE.

Who was he trying to kid?

We can be honest with each other?

He'd already shaded the truth.

Steve lay in his bed in his suite, wondering if what he was contemplating was wise. He hadn't been able to sleep at all tonight, thinking of Kelly just a wall away. At eight, he'd call Dimi and tell him the wedding was on.

When Kelly had opened that door tonight and he'd seen her in that dress, she had knocked him out as surely as if she'd punched him in the gut with her fist. It had been a long time since he'd had such a response to a woman. Since he'd hit, one of the unfortunate results had been an increased suspiciousness around people. It seemed that everyone wanted a piece of him.

Kelly, however, had been refreshingly honest about what piece of him she wanted—his approval of her script.

He'd thought she was a wacko little charmer, an amusing little girl, until he'd opened that door.

Luis, I owe you one.

He likened the chemistry he felt for her to a nuclear meltdown. The entire time they'd been in the limo on the way to The White Orchid, he'd been wondering how he could get her into bed.

A wild weekend between the sheets. A good time. No regrets.

Then he'd been shocked when every animal, male instinct he possessed had gone into possessive overdrive at the sight of Dimitri Alexandros lighting up like a Christmas tree at the sight of her.

After Kelly had left, Dimi had lit up one of his infamous cigars, puffed on it a few times, then gestured with it toward Steve.

"How badly do you want that woman?" he'd asked softly.

"Don't do this, Dimi," he'd replied, the words out of his mouth before he'd fully thought through the ramifications.

Later, he'd wondered at how he'd put everything on the line in order to protect her. He'd rationalized what he'd done, telling himself that Kelly would have been eaten alive in Dimi's jet-setting world of wealth and power. She wouldn't have stood a chance.

Dimi, perhaps suspecting he was being set up, had called his bluff.

"If you love her that much, let me arrange a wedding for the two of you. It would give me great pleasure to make that little one happy."

He'd known exactly what Dimi was doing, and for a moment had felt he didn't have a chance against this man. Then, his natural bravado had asserted itself, and he'd agreed.

"As long as Kelly wants it, too."

"If she loves you," Dimi had replied softly, "why would she not?"

He wants her. He's testing us. He's wondering if he can find a way to get her.

Dimitri Alexandros wasn't a wicked man, or even especially terrible. He was wealthy enough that when he saw someone, something, that caught his attention, he wanted it. Now. The women he'd loved spoke well of him, he usually left them very well-off. His prowess as a lover was legendary.

So why did you do it? Why not let Kelly take her chances with Dimi? He could buy her little sister an entire new body, let alone heart surgery.

But he couldn't, and he hadn't. First of all, he couldn't see Kelly agreeing to be a mistress. She needed the security of marriage and family.

Yeah, like what you're offering her is a hell of a lot better.

But it was. He wouldn't touch her. As much as he wanted to, he wouldn't. Because something had told him, halfway through his private conversation with Dimitri, that Kelly was still Kelly, glittery dress or not. Underneath the makeup, she was still frighteningly naive. She didn't truly understand this business or the people who chose to take part in it.

She was naive enough to still believe in miracles, while he'd been in the business long enough to know there was no such thing.

And, strangely enough, the one thing he was absolutely sure of was that Dimitri wouldn't go after Kelly if she was a married woman. Proud of his Greek heritage, Dimitri revered the family. It was part of his personal code of honor that he had never had an affair with a married woman.

Steve shifted uncomfortably on the large bed. You could lie to anyone else, but you couldn't lie to yourself—not for long—and still respect yourself in the morning. Maybe part of it was protecting her from Dimitri, but another part of it was that he wanted her for himself.

Of course there was the chance she was even more clever than he was giving her credit for. What if her entire persona was an act, designed to get under his skin and bamboozle him? What if she was simply another frustrated actress on the make who thought he held the key to her cinematic success?

But his instincts told him Kelly was for real. He didn't want to believe she could have simply concocted a story like that. Because if there was one thing he understood with complete and utter clarity, it was family loyalty.

Not wanting to examine his emotions too closely, Steve chose to concentrate on the protection angle, but that offered him no relief, either.

So you're going to protect her. Save her. Like you did such a good job last time....

He slid out of bed and walked over to the built-in bar. Anything to avoid the path his thoughts were taking. Pouring himself a shot of straight Scotch, he walked over toward the balcony and slid the glass door open. The ocean breeze cooled his overheated skin, and as he sipped his drink, he glanced over to the balcony next to his.

She was only a room away.

Downing the rest of the liquor in one swallow, he turned around, went back into his room, set the glass down on a table and headed for a cold shower.

KELLY CALLED her Aunt Bette at six in the morning and spilled the beans.

"So we get married, sell the pictures, I send you the money, Colleen gets her operation, Steve gets the part and I get my screenplay read." Rattling it off like that, it sounded exhausting.

"Honey," her aunt said worriedly, her Southern accent warm and rich, "I don't want you doin' anything with this man just to get some money." She paused. "But I can't imagine being around Steve Delany and not wanting to do somethin'." Her low chuckle sounded so wonderfully familiar to Kelly.

"No, it's not like that. It's one of those marriage of conveniences, like Andie McDowell and Gérard Dépardieu in *Green Card*."

"I remember that one, but you've got a better-lookin' man. Darlin', will you be able to stand it, being around such a hunk of man and not layin' a hand on him?"

"Bette!"

Her aunt laughed. "I keep forgettin', honey, you're not as wise to the ways of the world as I am. I want you to be careful, okay?"

"I will. But tell Colleen the minute she wakes up."

"I promise. When's the weddin'?"

"In the next couple of days." She took a deep breath. "Dimitri Alexandros is going to arrange everything."

"Dimitri Alexandros? Isn't he the one who made Onassis look like he was headed for the poorhouse?"

"The one and only."

"Oh, darlin' child, you be careful. What if it's some sort of white slavery thing or somethin'? But I can't see Nick Derringer doin' a thing like that."

"I can't see Steve doing that—"

"Oh, I just *love* the way you call him Steve! Is he just as cute in person?"

"Better."

"My, my, my. Be careful, honey."

"You think I'm doing the right thing?"

"If your instincts tell you you can trust him, then I think you're doin' each other a favor. Just don't let that man sweet-talk you into doin' anything you don't want to do."

"I know what you're talking about, Bette. I'll be careful."

But as she hung up the phone, Kelly wondered what she was letting herself in for.

LAST, BUT CERTAINLY NOT least, Steve tossed her a small, black box and said, "You might as well put this on and make it official."

She'd opened the box and looked straight at a huge diamond engagement ring. Then she'd blurted out the first thing that came into her mind.

"I can't wear this."

"What?"

"Wasn't this Pam's ring?"

"Well—"

"She picked it out, didn't she?"

"Yes, but—"

"And diamonds..."

"Yes?" She could tell he was struggling to follow her train of thought.

"I don't want a diamond—they're bad luck."

"Kelly, you're being unreasonable."

"But don't you see? No woman likes to wear another woman's ring. That'd be double bad luck."

"Bad luck? This isn't even a real marriage—"

"Exactly. We're tempting the Fates by playing with the concept of marriage as it is."

He'd looked supremely masculine and self-confident as he'd strode up to her side. Looking down at her with an expression of pure indulgence, he'd said, "Come on, Kelly. Just forget Pam and put it on."

Half an hour later, they were at Bernard Hurtig's jewelry store, picking out a new ring.

Kelly would have chosen a fabulous fake, but Steve told her that Dimi could spot a phony diamond a mile away.

"Could I get jade, instead?"

"What's jade? Good luck?"

"As a matter of fact—"

"Get whatever you want."

She picked an exquisite engagement ring of antique jade, and then they selected matching wedding bands. Their salesman, a tiny Oriental man named Ray, was most helpful and solicitous.

Once the jewelry was paid for, Kelly slipped her new engagement ring on while Ray carefully boxed their wedding bands. They spent the rest of the afternoon and early evening shopping for their wedding.

Kelly had spoken to Dimi over the phone and he'd told her to pick out whatever flowers she preferred at the hotel's florist.

She asked Steve what he liked, and the two of them compromised on lush, tropical blooms. Kelly maintained a cautious and conservative manner with their wedding flowers until Steve told her Dimi would be insulted unless they went all out.

Their wedding flowers made the salesgirl's day, week and month combined. There was bouquet after bouquet of anthuriums, brilliant red Indonesian wax ginger, bird of paradise and orchids—more orchids than Kelly had ever seen in her life. She loved their exotic-sounding colors. Pearl white, royal purple, blush white, aloha yellow, lavender supreme... The list was endless.

More and more flowers were added. Red torch, pink torch, pink ginger, red ginger, red banana, lavender banana, until she couldn't even remember what they'd first ordered.

But what touched her the most was the hibiscus blossom Steve bought her. White, with a pale pink center, it sat in its clear box, a pink ribbon wrapped around it and tied in a jaunty bow.

"What's that for?"

"You'll wear it over your right ear during the ceremony, then switch it to the left afterward. Over your left ear, it means you're a married woman."

"Just like in *Pardon My Sarong*. And *Flower of Nabonga*. That part where he says, 'Nabonga is angry, he will make the volcano erupt—'"

"—at least we have something in common. Bad taste in movies."

They capped their plunge into total decadence and extravagance by ordering three white orchid leis—one for each of them, and one for Dimitri.

"Will Donnatello be at the wedding?" Kelly asked nervously.

"Donnatel*l*a. Donnatello is one of the Ninja Turtles."

"Donnatel*l*a. Will she be there?"

"I doubt it. Dimitri tries to keep her away from people. She'll probably wait at the hotel, if she's here on the island at all."

Their shopping spree continued throughout the day. A pair of elegant slacks and a brilliant, royal blue Hawaiian shirt for Steve. A sarong-style dress, splashed with bright, salmon-colored blooms for her. High-heeled sandals that still didn't bring her up to his shoulders.

"You're sure we're not dressing too casually?" she asked him, as they loaded more packages into Dimi's waiting limousine. Marco had accompanied them on their shopping spree, waiting by the long, expensive car like an obedient puppy.

"There's an old saying in Hawaii. Roughly translated, it goes something like, 'When a man wears a suit, he's either going for a loan or he's a lawyer trying a case.' I think what we've picked out is just fine."

"But we dressed up last night."

"That was different. That was for Dimi."

"Oh."

After their shopping expedition, they asked Marco to drive them to Chinatown, where they chose a restaurant and sat at an outdoor table, eating fried noodles and beef in oyster sauce. Kelly could barely get her food down; she kept turning her head to see lei stands, herb shops, noodle factories and acupuncture studios. Fresh fish, exotic fruits and vegetables were all on display, and she couldn't take it all in.

They were barely finished with their meal when a male voice behind Kelly called out, "Hey, aren't you that Danger Guy?"

A fat man wearing a Hawaiian shirt with neon-orange blossoms, cutoff jeans, dark shoes and white socks came up and clapped Steve on the back. "Nick Danger! I remember you!" The tourist had a camera around his neck, and the buttons on his shirt were straining against his generous beer belly.

Kelly glanced around. Behind her stood the wife and three children, looking embarrassed and hopeful.

Steve rose to the occasion. "Derringer. Nick Danger is a "Firesign Theater" character."

"That's where I got it! Derringer, right! Always just in the nick of time!" The man laughed loudly, pleased

at his own joke. "Hey, Nick, would you mind—could
I get a picture?"

"Sure." Steve stood up, and right before Kelly's
eyes he seemed to turn into Nick Derringer, private
eye. He flirted with the wife and she blushed profusely, the expression in her eyes quietly thrilled. He
teased the children, and soothed the fears of the lit-
tlest. He even perched the little girl up on his shoulders for one of the pictures, and by this time she was
laughing with delight.

A small crowd gathered to see what the commotion
was about, and it was almost forty-five minutes later
before Steve made a graceful exit and they made their
way back to Marco and the limousine.

"You're very good at that," she remarked, once
they were on their way back to the hotel.

"Hey, why be a jerk about it? These people made
the show popular. Why would I want to let them
down?"

"I liked the way you kind of turned into Nick Derringer."

"That's what they want. I learned pretty early on
that it's not wise to mess with people's fantasies. They
don't want me, they want Nick, and that's okay."

She directed her gaze out the window, but didn't see
the lush, green tropical foliage or the brilliant blossoms. There had been several female fans in the group,
most of whom had asked Steve to autograph various
parts of their anatomy. She'd been surprised and annoyed with herself at how it had rankled her.

She had no right to be jealous; she wasn't really his
fiancée. And she didn't suppose anything was going to

change once she was his make-believe wife. Still, you couldn't stop strong emotion, and she was wise enough not to try and make up stories to fool herself.

Back in her room, she hung up the sarong next to her sequined evening dress, unpacked her shoes, then kicked her rubber thongs off and flung herself down on the bed. Impulsively, she dialed her family.

Aunt Bette answered on the third ring, and Kelly filled her in on the shopping trip, the rings, the flowers, lunch with Steve, the autographing session and how wonderful Hawaii was.

"Maybe when all this is over and Colleen feels better, the three of us can take a trip."

"That sounds good, honey. Colleen's asleep, or I'd call her to the phone."

"Don't wake her up. Just give her a kiss for me when she gets up."

Both women had already decided that it was too exhausting and risky for Colleen to travel. Neither she nor Bette would attend the wedding, but Bette had extracted a bizarre promise from Kelly. She wanted her niece to videotape the wedding and send her a copy so she could play it and see everything.

"My cousin Patty's going to split a gut when she finds out Nick Derringer's my nephew by marriage— even if it is only temporary."

"Don't tell her the truth—"

"*Never!* According to what I know, it was a love match from the git-go." She paused. "And if the marriage is tempestuous, just think what fun we'll have with the divorce!"

The two women chatted a little longer, then Kelly hung up and lay back down on the bed.

You're getting married tomorrow.

Well, not really.

But it was going to be a real ceremony, and by the end of the following day, the media would make sure that even Tibetan monks living in the farthest corners of the world would know that Nick Derringer, alias Steve Delany, had married Kelly Archer.

It was a strange feeling.

Bridal nerves?

Hah!

She wasn't a real bride, and there was absolutely no reason for her to be nervous. It wasn't as if she was going to share a bed with Steve tomorrow night. It wasn't as if, at twenty-three, she even had any idea of what sharing a bed with a man was all about.

That's me—Kelly Archer, professional virgin.

Her life hadn't left her a lot of time for that sort of stuff. If Kelly was honest with herself, she hadn't wanted it. Oh, she could have spent a lot of time in psychoanalysis and found out that she had a total and all-consuming fear of abandonment because of her father dying when she was a child and her mother dying several years later.

Kelly preferred to simplify things. She was scared spitless.

Though her personality was a tad on the impulsive side, inside she was a bundle of mush. Shy. Insecure. Until Luis had been given free rein with her.

That night had been magical, she'd felt like a different person. Attractive. Alluring. Frisky.

Then she'd taken off the dress and rinsed off the makeup and metamorphosed into Kelly the pumpkin.

Face it, she thought as she lay on the bed and stared at the ceiling, *you'll never fit into Steve's world. Not really.*

A saying of her aunt's filtered into her thoughts.

Fake it 'til you make it.

Could she do it? Could she pull this entire charade off? Would Dimitri suspect that by the time they got married, she and Steve would have known each other for only a few days?

She'd taken some acting classes while learning to write screenplays, and because of that experience, a completely new idea flashed into her mind. She could view this entire experience as a part in a play!

And what a part it was! How many women got to marry a man who set women's hearts all around the world fluttering like crazy? How many women—or men, for that matter—ever got a chance to see how the other half really lived?

How hard could it possibly be, to go along with Steve's crazy scheme and have the time of her life?

DON'T GIVE HER A CHANCE to change her mind.

Steve paced his suite restlessly, glancing at the wall that separated him from Kelly. Though he'd spent the entire day with her, and practically run her legs off, those long, long legs . . .

Get your mind off the girl.

He didn't want her to have too much time alone to think about what they were going to do.

It was absolutely insane, but he was determined that this whole scheme was going to work.

He'd wanted this part from the beginning. Dimitri specialized in action-adventure extravaganzas, and this particular part wasn't that big a stretch from his character in "The Nick of Time." If he could pull off the part of Rick Durran, soldier of fortune, he'd leave detective Nick Derringer behind in the dust forever.

But Kelly had thrown that interesting little wrench into the works.

He wanted to get involved with her. That glittery dress had turned him into a seething testosterone bomb. Those gloves had called attention to her delicate hands, and all the places he'd like them to touch. And he didn't even want to start thinking about the fantasies he'd woven about her long, long legs....

He wanted to get involved with her, but he wasn't quite sure how to go about it. She was unlike any woman he'd ever met, and he seriously doubted that she'd go for the idea of a quickie affair, lack of movie theaters or not.

Take her out on a date. Don't leave her alone. Don't let her think too much.

The one thing that Steve had learned during his years of struggling was that everyone had a weakness.

And I'll find hers.

THE BRISK KNOCK on her door could only be one person, and she found her heart picking up speed as she got up off the bed and started toward the suite's door.

She swung it open and came face-to-face with her fake fiancé.

"I'm taking you out on a date."

That smile again. Only this time it didn't look like a Nick Derringer smile for the camera. It looked like a genuine, Steve Delany smile. Just for her.

You're falling fast....

"A date?"

"I thought we should have one bona fide date before we got married. If we do, it's got to be tonight."

"Dimi got the license?"

He nodded.

You'll be married to this man by tomorrow night....

Her heart was doing strange things to her equilibrium. Her mind was making all sorts of rationalizations as to why she should go through with it. Her hormones were on overdrive.

The strange thing is, he'd make a terrific husband. Stop it, Kelly. Get a grip on that imagination.

The truth was, she was falling in love.

And that could be, emotionally, the most dangerous truth of all.

Chapter Four

She couldn't remember having more fun on a date.

Actually, she hadn't been on that many dates. Dating was a funny thing in Hollywood, quite unlike anywhere else in the world.

The first cut occurred when everyone asked you what you did. If you had an inconsequential job or didn't fit into the industry in any way, you were out.

The second cut involved beauty. There was a funny theory she'd heard, that people in Southern California were so beautiful because so many of their parents and grandparents had come out west to be movie stars. Something along the lines of, "You're so beautiful, you should be in pictures!" Those that hadn't made it had gone forth into the bright sunshine, been fruitful and multiplied. Whatever the explanation, there was an astounding amount of natural beauty in the city.

The third cut had been in her own mind. Some of the men she'd dated had been as ambitious as she'd been. They'd thought she was there simply for a little sex, some free typing, editing and fixing coffee. A glorified girl Friday. She'd thought of what Rosalind

Russell in *His Girl Friday* would have done, and caught on fast. When she hadn't been particularly agreeable to their game plans, the relationships hadn't lasted long.

She'd been both blindingly shy and blazingly ambitious. It had been a strange combination, guaranteed to prevent her from being a social butterfly.

The men she'd really liked had been honest with her. She'd gone out with a surfer for a while; they'd spent what little free time each of them had, swimming in the ocean and lying out in the sun. Then she'd met a musician. He'd been a drummer in a local group, and had told her he only wanted a fling. But she was "too nice a girl," whatever that meant these days. Fresh-faced and all that.

A regular Doris Day.

She'd wondered if that was the way Steve saw her.

He'd picked her up in his own car, a red Ferrari. She was kind of glad the ever-present Marco wouldn't be chaperoning them. For just this one night, she wanted to forget that Dimitri Alexandros was involved in their relationship.

They'd driven around for a while, and he'd let her decide what they would do for the evening.

Kelly had wanted to be cool and sophisticated, a knowledgeable woman of the world. But this was going to be kind of hard to pull off, considering she'd never visited Hawaii before and had no idea what the nightlife here was like. So she turned the entire evening over to Steve.

He liked that. A lot. And she made a mental note to herself that she'd have to get a little more assertive in this make-believe marriage. Steve Delany was a nice guy, but, like Dimi, he hadn't gotten to where he was by being a cream puff.

Once he found out she adored Japanese food, Steve took her to the Pearl City Tavern. It was a bit of a drive, but Kelly couldn't remember when she'd enjoyed a car trip more. Steve was an excellent traveling companion, he handled his sportscar with that natural cockiness that was so much a part of his character. But he wasn't reckless.

The Pearl City Tavern was clearly a local hangout. Steve pointed out the famous Monkey Bar, with live monkeys behind glass panels. The decorations were Japanese, down to the bonsai garden upstairs.

He'd insisted that she dress casual, and this place certainly made her feel totally comfortable. Even though he was a world-famous television star, they were on one of the most beautiful islands in the world and they were entering a marriage of convenience in the morning, this could have passed for a regular date.

Almost.

Steve seemed preoccupied, and she wondered if he were already regretting this impulsive date.

"So how did you get started?"

"What?" Kelly said, puzzled at the sudden question.

"Writing. How did you get started writing?"

"I used to make up bedtime stories for my sister so she'd fall asleep—not that I want my stories to put people to sleep."

He was smiling at her and, encouraged, she continued.

"And she kept asking for more of them, so I kept making them up. Then one day she suggested I write a book. So I did."

"Where is it?"

"Under my bed. And it's never going to see daylight."

"What's it about?"

"Vampires. But that's not why it's never going to see daylight."

"Vampires?"

"They take over this studio and, eventually, Hollywood."

"Ah, an exposé. I love stories that are true to life." She laughed.

"I'd like to read it."

"Oh, no."

"Bad?"

"There aren't words to describe it."

He laughed then, and she found herself liking the sound.

"Why screenplays?"

"What else is there to do in Los Angeles? No, actually I took a class at UCLA and got hooked." She decided to change the subject. "How did you decide on acting?"

"What else is there to do in Los Angeles? This screenplay you left in my room, it's not about vampires is it?"

"Nope." She smiled. "Except for the agent. Just kidding."

"Art imitates life. What's it about?"

"It's a thriller. A young woman submits a screenplay to a major studio, and everything she wrote starts to happen to her. It's kind of—suspenseful."

Not half as suspenseful as this dinner.

She couldn't stop looking at him. He was flirting with her and she knew it, but Kelly felt safe within the confines of the deal they had made. She couldn't stop her smile.

"What? What are you thinking?"

"I can't believe I'm having dinner with the sexiest man alive."

"Don't start that stuff."

"You don't like it?"

"It gets in the way of the work."

"It's better than the alternative."

He laughed.

"Did you read the survey in that women's magazine about you and a desert island?" Kelly asked.

"My agent read me the pertinent parts."

"I think it's pretty flattering."

"If the women of America could see me before I have my first cup of coffee in the morning, they'd run screaming."

I'm sure. This man has made stubble into an art form.

She decided to tease him.

"I liked last year's survey."

"Oh, *please—*"

"No, just think about it for a second. It's mind-boggling. Eighty-seven percent of American women chose you as their top choice to fantasize about while they're making love to their husbands."

"It's an awesome responsibility."

She grinned. "I'm sure you never let them down."

If looks could kill...

The look he was giving her was pure, deadly Derringer. But Kelly knew she was as safe as if she were his little sister's best friend.

Later in the evening, as they drove back to Honolulu, she wondered at how skillfully he'd kept the conversation away from anything really personal about himself.

What she knew about him, she knew from the various newspaper and magazine interviews she'd read during her research. He was one of four children, his parents lived in Oregon. The whole family was thrilled with his success, he loved to get away and spend time in his small hometown by the ocean. Steve had nieces and nephews, and someday looked forward to having a family of his own.

Perfect family. Perfect star. Perfect man.

"The only thing wrong with Japanese food," Steve said, breaking into her thoughts, "is that they never have good desserts."

"They're very healthy people."

"Don't you want some sugar?"

"Lead on."

"I'll surprise you."

He began to enchant her then. When they reached Honolulu, Steve pulled up outside a little Italian café just off the beach. Within minutes he brought back two pieces of vanilla cheesecake with mango sauce.

"The guy makes the sauce from the fruit on his own tree."

She took a bite of the rich dessert, then closed her eyes in sheer bliss. This, all of this, was such a rare treat. There had been times in the past couple of years when she'd wondered if she'd forgotten how to have fun. She had a feeling that Steve was a person who chose to have a lot of fun, wherever he was and whatever he did.

They walked on the beach afterward, keeping in sight of the high-rise hotels. And Kelly thought she would never grow tired of the sighing of the ocean, the gentle wind, the scents of flowers she was only now beginning to recognize.

It was so terribly romantic, and her romantic's heart wished desperately that Steve would fall a little bit in love with her. But, remembering what he'd told her about Donnatella and the wild weekend in the small Italian village, Kelly knew it was all wishful thinking. She wasn't his type. Not at all.

They walked back to the hotel and took the elevator back up to their floor. He walked her to her door, and she fumbled in her purse for her room key. The thought of their evening together ending was suddenly sad to her, and she spoke without thinking.

"You can come in, if you want."

The sudden, tense silence told her what she'd just said. She hadn't meant it that way, but Kelly realized that a part of her, the deeply emotional part of her, wouldn't have objected. The thought of Steve Delany being her first lover was overwhelming—but so exciting.

"I'd better not." His voice was low, almost rough, and it seemed to her he was deliberately pulling away.

She had to salvage the moment. She didn't want their magical evening to end this way.

"For coffee, I meant." Her door was open now, and she stepped partially through the threshold. "I just—I'm a little nervous about tomorrow."

"Don't be." He hesitated for a moment, then followed her inside.

She called down to room service and ordered up a pot of coffee, then kicked off her sandals and wiggled her toes in the thick, plush rug. Kelly caught Steve watching her, then he grinned.

"What's so funny?"

"You. You're cute, the way you enjoy things."

Cute. Doris Day is cute. Poodles are cute. Babies and kittens are cute.

Donnatella Marciano isn't cute. Sultry, sexy, devastating—but not cute.

She didn't want to be cute, she wanted to be a woman of the world. But she wasn't. Kelly knew she was a strange combination of both the romantic and the intensely practical, with a little bit of the spiritual thrown in. She'd just have to be what she was.

"Mind if I turn on the television?" he asked.

"Go ahead."

The eleven o'clock news was just starting, and the dark-haired newscaster looked jubilant.

"Our top story tonight concerns the wedding plans of actor Steve Delany—"

"What!" Steve said.

Simultaneously, Kelly turned and stared at the screen.

"—and Ray here has all the details."

Transfixed, she watched as Ray, the solicitous salesclerk at the jewelry store, told viewers that they had bought rings from him, that Steve Delany had actually stood in this store. Then he went on to elaborate: what kind of rings, and how much in love they'd seemed.

Then there was a nice little chat with the hotel florist, concerning what kind of flowers they'd ordered and how they were going to be arranged.

Then there was general speculation by one and all as to where the wedding was to take place. And was there any truth to the rumors that multimillionaire Dimitri Alexandros was involved? Had Kelly been his mistress? Was she his daughter?

"I can't believe this!" she said.

"I can," Steve said softly, his eyes never leaving the screen. He seemed angry.

Their coffee arrived, and she directed their waiter to the small table between two overstuffed chairs. Thankfully, even with the television on and both of them clearly staring at the news report, the young man remained professional and extremely discreet as he went about his business. She'd just closed the door after him when she heard the newscaster say, "And now a look at where this mystery woman actually came from."

They knew her name. Where she was from. That she was on vacation and had "obviously met Steve" while on her trip. No, she hadn't met him before to anyone's knowledge. And yes, she was from Los Angeles, as a matter of fact....

"That's my apartment building!" she yelped.

The small, stucco building looked painfully plain on the television screen. The camera held steady as the newscaster's voice droned on and on. Where she'd gone to school, where she'd worked—every detail they could think to dredge up.

It left her feeling emotionally naked.

"How do they know all this?" she asked Steve, a hint of desperation in her voice.

And then, her aunt's duplex in Hollywood. Reporters were crowded around the front porch, then Bette appeared in the doorway, dressed in a snazzy suit she'd probably found in a secondhand store on Melrose. Only, on Bette, it looked like a Chanel.

"Gentlemen, gentlemen, please!" Her smoky Southern accent practically demanded civilized behavior. And the amazing thing was, she got it.

"Now, I'll answer some questions for y'all, but not if you're going to behave like a bunch of animals!"

Steve leaned back in his chair, a bemused grin on his face. Kelly handed him a cup of coffee, then couldn't help smiling. If there was anyone who could salvage this situation, it was her aunt.

"Where did they meet?" A reporter tried to stick his mike in her face.

"Darlin', if you're going to stick something in my face, it better have whipped cream on it!" Bette looked directly at the camera, completely comfortable in the public eye. "I talked to my niece just this mornin', and I believe she said she met that nice Mr. Delany on the beach."

"They hadn't met before?"

Bette laughed, a deep, rich sound, filled with some private amusement. "No, sir, I don't believe they did."

"And the wedding—"

"—Will be private, as far as I can tell. Very romantic, don't you think?"

"Isn't this all kind of sudden?"

"The best kind of love always is, sugar." Bette winked at the reporter, and Steve started to laugh.

"She's a natural," he said. "And she sounds just like Elizabeth Ashley."

"She acts just like her, too."

"Why do you think Steve Delany fell in love with your niece?" another reporter demanded.

"Why not? She's a *very* nice girl." At this, Bette looked straight into the camera again, only this time Kelly had the distinct impression it was for Steve's benefit, if he should be watching the telecast.

"But what is it that's special about Kelly Archer?"

"She's my niece, that's special enough. Now, gentlemen, you're simply *ruining* my flower beds, and I'm going to have to ask y'all to come back another time—"

The newscast veered off in another direction, and Kelly quietly sipped her coffee, wondering what Steve thought about what her aunt had said.

"She handled it very well."

Kelly hadn't realized she was holding her breath until she felt herself letting it out, slowly.

"She means well."

"No, she did a great job. If Dimi watched the news tonight, we're home free."

"Oh." Of course he would think of Dimitri's reaction. After all, that's what this whole thing was about, wasn't it? Still, Kelly could feel that little bit of yearning building inside of her, and she couldn't seem to stop it from happening.

He looked so handsome, so vital, so terribly alive, sitting in that chair and drinking his coffee. His attention was no longer on the news; he was looking at her, and Kelly thought she'd never seen such a handsome man in all her life.

Why can't I just be impartial about this? Why can't I just look on it as a business deal and stop imagining it were something more? Why do I have to be so emotional about everything?

She couldn't help it. She was cursed with a writer's brain.

Though Kelly thought of herself as a practical woman, she'd always done what she had to do to survive. But when push came to shove, her heart overruled her head. Every time.

This time, she had to keep her heart—and her overactive imagination—under control.

"Feeling a little less nervous?"

"What?" She set her coffee down and tried to collect her thoughts. It was an occupational hazard with writers, always thinking about something else while in the midst of whatever was going on.

"About tomorrow."

"Oh. Yes." She sat down on the chair across from him and pretended to concentrate on the weather report. Perfect weather expected for tomorrow, high in the seventies.

Perfect weather for her wedding.

"I've asked Dimitri to be our best man," Steve said. Kelly brought her attention back around to him. Sometimes it seemed as if just looking at him gave her an emotional overload. She was going to have to be very careful not to ever let him see her real feelings.

They had another cup of coffee, chatted about inconsequential things, then Steve got up to leave. For one wild moment, Kelly thought of asking him to call the whole thing off, then she steeled her mind against the fear threatening to take over.

It had already been put in motion. Dimitri had been put to too much trouble. She needed the money the tabloid pictures would bring. Colleen needed the money.

For her heart. For a chance.

She walked Steve to the door and watched him cross the short distance to his suite. And as he closed his door, Kelly knew there was nothing she wouldn't do for her little sister.

Including marrying a man eighty-seven percent of the women of America made love to every night.

KELLY SAT on her balcony, watching the sunrise bathe the sky with the most incredible colors. Soft purples, pinks and golds. It was a gift, watching such beauty on her wedding day. And it was soothing, knowing there was something larger than her own life, some force greater than herself. Sitting in the lotus position, Kelly tried to still her mind.

A difficult thing to do, on the morning of her wedding.

Meditating every morning had helped center her in so many ways. This morning she felt so very out of control.

Was it right, what she was doing? This marriage was a form of deception, a taking advantage of Dimitri on one level.

Sometimes it did no good to fight the thoughts that came into consciousness, and this morning Kelly didn't even try.

A Buddhist truth flitted into her mind. Right actions produce a natural calm. Wrongful actions produce guilt and fear.

But could it be wrong, to want more for her sister? Parties and dating and marriage and babies—everything, all of it, the best of everything.

She'd known what she was promising her mother when she'd agreed to take care of Colleen, but she hadn't hesitated, not for a second.

They took care of each other, she and Colleen. Spirit and heart, fire and water, two parts of the same whole.

She thought of Steve.

It's not love, it's just that he's been good to you. That's all it is, nothing more....

In her heart, she knew it wasn't true.

You must refrain from taking what is not given....

Another Buddhist truth, and a great one. How simple to understand, how hard to enact in the real world.

Steve wasn't giving her love, he was giving her protection. He was giving her this marriage as a means of making the money Colleen would need to have a chance at something beyond an invalid's life. He was also giving her script a chance.

In return, she was giving him the chance of a lifetime, the opportunity to climb to even greater heights, the chance to be able to pick and choose his projects. The artist's ultimate dream.

Don't fail him.

The sunrise was fading into a brilliant wash of blue. The ocean glittered beneath her, stretching out as far as the eye could see. As calmness descended over her, Kelly knew she was making the right choice, the correct choice, the only choice.

Now there was no turning back.

"Thank you, Luis."

The woman who gazed back at her in the mirror was truly beautiful.

Luis had opted to keep her hair down, with only Steve's hibiscus bloom to adorn it. The makeup he'd applied was light, natural looking and completely waterproof.

"In case you cry, *chérie.*"

"I won't...I don't..." She fumbled for words, hating her gaucheness, wondering how much he knew and if she should even be letting him know anything about what was really going on. But he'd known about Pam, and he knew she hadn't known Steve long, and how could he think anything except that this whole setup was a little strange?

He stilled her nervousness by placing a comforting hand on her bare shoulder. She was sitting in front of the vanity in her sarong, Luis was standing behind her and now her eyes met his in the mirror.

"I know more than you think I do, *chérie*."

She couldn't meet his gaze, wondering what he must think of her. Did he know the entire story, why she had to go through with this?

"Luis, I know what you must think of me—"

"No, you do not." He pulled a chair up beside her and sat down on it, his usually smiling face alert and intense. As he spoke to her, his hands were busy with little last-minute adjustments to her hair and makeup.

"I want you to know something about Steve. You think you know the real Steve Delany, the world thinks it knows who he is. You're both wrong."

Of all the things he could have said, this surprised her the most. His words shocked her into silence; she simply looked at him, her expression asking for a certain amount of clarification.

"But what . . . then what is he?"

"I can't tell you. But I can tell you that he's a good man, and he needs you. More than he knows right now. But given time, he'll find out."

"But . . . but we're only going to be married for a short time, until—"

"I know. But it's never that simple, and it won't be that simple this time. Trust me."

She looked down at her hands, manicured to perfection, her nails glossed with a delicate shade of pink. The thought of Luis thinking badly about her upset her. He was her only friend in Hawaii, her confidant, and the need for confession rose up inside until it was almost choking her.

"Luis, I—"

"No, don't explain. Kelly, if I had a sister, I'd want her to be just like you."

He knows.

The knowledge brought tears to her eyes.

"No, don't cry. Not now, we don't want you going to the altar with a red nose." His hand was warm and reassuring on her back, and she blinked quickly, stemming the flow of emotion. Before she had a chance to hesitate, she threw her arms around him and hugged him fiercely. He hugged her back, and she could sense he was offering her his friendship on a deeper level.

"Luis?" she whispered.

"Yes?"

"Would you be my maid of honor?"

"Darling, I thought you'd never ask."

Chapter Five

The wedding went off without a hitch.

Almost.

Kelly had never read about any wedding like hers in *Bride Magazine.* Instead of fighting the craziness, she simply surrendered herself into Steve's protection.

Make sure to keep your makeup light and your hairstyle and veil simple, so the incredible rush of wind generated by the rotary blades from the helicopter won't turn you into a total disaster....

"We're going to the wedding in *what?*"

"The hotel's surrounded, Kel, there's no other way out."

"But I'm scared of heights!"

Understand that your husband probably has a past, that there may be several women who will feel quite badly that he is now no longer an eligible bachelor....

"There are thousands of women down there!"

"And I didn't have affairs with any of them."

You'll understandably be quite nervous on your wedding day. Don't let a little attack of the jitters spoil what should be one of the most memorable occasions of your life.

"Steve, I'm going to be sick—"

"Don't look down."

The choice of your wedding photographer is crucial, as he will be recording this most precious day....

The photographer from the *National Star* was British, barefoot, wore tight pants and an unbuttoned shirt and had bad teeth. He took so many pictures while the beachfront ceremony proceeded that Kelly wondered if they were going to publish a special issue devoted entirely to Nick Derringer's wedding.

" . . . And if there is anyone here who objects to this union, let them speak now or forever hold their—"

"Aughhhhhhhhh!!!" The photographer had dropped his expensive camera in the sand and was hopping up and down on one foot, furiously kicking the other while trying to dislodge an equally furious sand crab.

The ceremony came to a screeching halt.

Everyone followed the photographer's progress until Dimitri turned to the flustered and intimidated minister.

"There are no objections. Please continue."

"Umm, ahh, oh, yes—what God hath joined together, let no man tear asunder—"

"Hurry it up," Dimitri growled.

"Kiss the bride," the minister squeaked. "Now."

Steve complied. Her "no tongues" request was completely forgotten as Kelly discovered that eighty-seven percent of America's women had the right idea.... And this was only a kiss!

When she came up for air, she was afraid she was going to get the bends. But before she could dwell on her own feelings, the photographer intruded with a few of his own.

"Bloody 'ell!" he squawked. "I get a crab on my foot and the two of you kiss! You promised me a kiss for the cover, and I want it...*now!*"

Steve turned toward the disgruntled man and flashed him a killer grin. "No problem." He turned toward Kelly and took her into his arms, à la Clark Gable and Vivien Leigh in that famous pose on the *Gone With the Wind* poster.

And kissed her again.

No, it's not the bends...it's rapture of the deep.

They broke the kiss and the photographer was practically in tears.

"The bloody film jammed!"

"No problem."

As Kelly went down for the third time, she thought hazily, What a way to go....

LATER, during the reception, everyone contributed their ideas for next week's *National Star* headline.

"Crabs Crab Derringer Wedding," quipped Luis as he reached for more beluga caviar.

"Or how about, Killer Alien Crustacean Destroys Derringer Marriage?" offered Kelly.

"No, I've got it," Steve said. "Photographer Catches Crabs At Derringer Lovefest."

They were all laughing so hard, they barely heard the beginning of a series of toasts. After Kelly's third glass of champagne, she was beyond worrying.

This, she thought happily, *is going to be a piece of cake. A piece of wedding cake.*

IN CHOOSING WHERE TO GO on your honeymoon, both budget and personal likes and dislikes should be taken into consideration. Don't choose a tropical island if your man likes to ski....

Dimitri waited until the wedding brunch was almost over before he dropped his bomb.

And what a bomb it was.

"May I have your attention, please." Dimitri easily commanded everyone's total concentration as he stood and held up his flute of champagne. Everyone at the table did the same, awaiting his toast.

"It has given me nothing but pleasure to arrange this wedding. I am a great lover of romance, and I believe in marriage, despite my two divorces."

No one said a word. Dimitri Alexandros was not the sort of man to whom one talked back.

"And so, it give me great pleasure to give Steve and Kelly their final gift."

"Dimi, we couldn't possibly—" Steve began.

Kelly glanced at her new husband. She sensed he was uneasy. But she had no idea how, in the space of a few seconds, Dimitri was going to totally screw up their lives.

If anyone was an expert at playing God, it was Dimi.

"And that final gift is that, as of today, I am going to delay starting production on my movie for three weeks, so that these two can have a proper honeymoon aboard my yacht, *The Aphrodite.*"

Kelly could feel her blood roaring in her ears. She glanced at Steve and noticed that he seemed to be turning a peculiar shade of pale.

It was impossible.

It was insane.

It couldn't be happening.

Kelly swallowed against the fear building inside of her. Nothing could be worse than what Dimitri had just announced.

"Of course," Dimitri continued, while everyone still held their champagne aloft, "I will be there, as well, as will Donnatella, and we shall spend several days discussing the intricacies of the script—"

Well, almost nothing.

Her instincts were working overtime, screaming at her that Dimi didn't believe that this marriage was real, and this so-called honeymoon was a perfect way to find out. Kelly thought back to the Emergency Broadcasting System messages that had played across her television screen in Los Angeles.

This is a test.

This is only a test.

The multimillionaires of your acquaintance, in compliance with crazy Greek ethics, have devised this test to warn you that if you're trying to pull a fast one, it's not going to work.

Kelly blinked her eyes rapidly against the sting of frightened tears. Dimi was going to find out.

And remember, if this were an actual emergency, you would already be dead.

A comforting thought.

And one to remember, should everything turn out the way she suspected it was going to.

LIKE FRIGHTENED BRIDES have done since the beginning of time—or at least since the beginning of indoor plumbing—Kelly locked herself in the bathroom that night.

"Kel, come on out. We've got to talk."

"This deal is totally out of control!"

"That's not entirely true."

"Oh, yeah? What are we supposed to do now, Steve? Take a honeymoon of convenience? I've never heard of a plot line like this one, and I've pitched some doozies!"

"Kel, calm down. We've got to talk."

"What's the point? We're doomed! He knows! He didn't believe it was a real engagement, he doesn't believe it's a real marriage and you're not going to get the part!"

"Hey, the hell with the part. At least you got the money for your sister, and that's more important."

The snick of the door unlocking sounded very loud in the absolute quiet of the bridal suite.

"You think so?" Kelly cautiously stuck her head out the door. She couldn't meet Steve's eyes.

"Yeah. I do."

"What are we going to do?"

"We have all night to think of something."

"What will...what will Dimi do if he finds out we're just friends?"

"Kill me and take off with you."

"What!" She couldn't believe what she was hearing.

"Kel, I haven't been entirely honest with you. Remember when he kissed your hand at the nightclub?"

"I thought he was just being continental."

"Nope. He fell for you."

"I didn't know—"

"I know you didn't know. It was another one of the reasons I thought this marriage idea would work. Dimi may be a ruthless kind of guy, but he does respect the institution of marriage. Unless, that is, he doesn't think it *is* a marriage."

"Like your engagement to Pam wasn't an engagement. Oh, God, I'm getting a migraine." She started out of the bathroom and began to pace the spacious suite.

"Kel, we can work this out."

"I'm scared. He's going to send some of his men after us."

"He's a Greek tycoon, not a Mafia kingpin!"

"Wouldn't you be scared if Dimi were after you?"

"I'd be amazed. He's always gone for women as far as I know."

"Don't joke. I mean, as a woman, wouldn't you be scared if you knew he was after you?"

"Yeah."

"Ohhhh..." She fell back on the king-size bed, closed her eyes and put a hand over them, curled up into a tight ball of misery and wondered if she could get away with having a complete and total nervous breakdown.

What a way to spend your wedding night.

"Look," Steve said, dropping down beside her on the bed. "We can salvage this. I think you're a good enough actress, and I know I can pull this off—"

"What's that supposed to mean?" Kelly knew she was being irrational, but she was too upset to care.

"What's what supposed to mean?"

"Am I that much of a dog that you have to psyche yourself up to even think that you might have looked at me as marriage material?"

"That's not what I meant."

"Then what did you mean?"

"I think you're amazingly attractive."

The world came to a complete and total standstill. Kelly took her hand away from her eyes, stared at Steve and tried to assimilate what he'd just said.

"You do?"

"Yes."

"Really?"

"Really."

"Well...I guess you should know... Oh, I can't tell you!"

"Kel. Kel, look at me. If we're going to have a chance in hell of pulling this thing off, we're going to have to be totally honest with each other. Starting right now."

She sat up on the large bed, eyeing him warily.

"Okay."

"Good. Now, what were you going to tell me?"

"Well, what I meant to say was—I mean, I'd have to be dead not to be attracted to you—just a little. And, I mean, I thought we were going to be able to do this wedding thing and then I was going to be able to fly home and only see you on television. But I don't know about being alone with you for twenty-one nights on a yacht in the middle of the ocean.... I mean, it's not a desert island, but eighty-seven percent of American women can't be all wrong.''

He stared at her for so long, she finally put her hands over her eyes and fell back down on the bed, totally embarrassed.

SHE'S ATTRACTED TO ME....

He couldn't believe it. This woman, this woman who had been driving him totally crazy since the moment he laid eyes on her—well, the second moment he'd laid eyes on her—was attracted to him.

Which could only lead to one thing.

Which was exactly what he wanted.

He started toward her, testosterone kicking into high gear. ''I don't think we have a problem then, Kelly. I mean, after all, we're married—''

''Yes we do,'' she said, her voice sounding all choked and fluttery. ''I mean, I'm not the sort of woman you usually throw yourself at. I'm not sophisticated and suave and in the know. I'll probably embarrass you on the yacht by using the wrong fork.''

''We'll eat with our fingers.''

''No, you don't get it.'' She darted out of his reach, danced around the bed, keeping herself just out of range. He looked so predatory, so virile, so very male as he zeroed in on her, and Kelly wondered if this was what it felt like to be stalked.

"Kel, I think we could really have something here...." He caught her arm, and she could feel herself weakening. What was it about this man?

"I'm still a virgin," she whispered miserably.

HE LET GO OF HER as if she'd burned him. "What?"

"You heard me."

"A virgin?"

"Don't say it so loud!"

"A *virgin!*"

"It's not a disease!"

"At least not an incurable one. I'm astounded. How old *are* you?"

"Twenty-three," she muttered.

"What?"

"I'm twenty-three!" she said defiantly. Kelly felt hopelessly inadequate and out of her league. This man had probably been sexually active since his Little League days. And here she was, the world's oldest living virgin married to America's most wanted....

"I'm sorry."

"For what?"

"For... being in this thing so over my head. For not knowing whether I can help you through this...honeymoon. Don't you understand, Steve? I wouldn't have any idea how a...sexually satisfied woman would behave."

"We could improvise."

She glared at him, frustration welling up inside her. "Very funny."

"No, that's not what I meant. I mean, I'll help you out as much as I can."

"What do you know about sexually satisfied women? Forget it. I forgot there probably weren't that many movie theaters at most of your film locations."

"I *knew* you were still burned about my affair with Donnatella."

"You've got to admit, if not for that, we wouldn't be in this mess."

"If you hadn't climbed on to my balcony—"

"If *you'd* been a little more available—"

"If *you* hadn't charmed Dimi—"

"Ohhhh!"

He took hold of her upper arms then, and she started at his touch, amazed at her reaction to his fingers against her bare skin. It was as if no one had ever really touched her before. Slowly she looked up into his eyes and became very still at the expression in them.

They both studied each other for a long, tension-filled moment, then Steve shook his head slightly as if to clear it and stared down at her.

"It's happening, Kelly. We're not going to make it if we fight. Dimi's going to win, and I don't want that to happen."

The thought of Dimitri Alexandros coming after her was a frightening one, and in a reflex action, Kelly wound her arms around Steve's neck and stepped closer to him.

His arms came around her then, warm and strong. Comforting. She rested her head against his shirt-front, could hear the strong beating of his heart, could smell the scent that was distinctly his.

She couldn't think. She couldn't make any sense out of her reaction to this man. She could only feel.

It crossed her mind, in one of the few brief lucid moments in his arms, that the last man who had held her this gently had been her father.

His touch soothed her, and she knew then that she couldn't let him down. She had to help him. They had to fool Dimitri. It went beyond being scared of the millionaire's attraction to her. It was simply that Steve deserved a break, and she wanted to help him with his career the same way he was helping her with her own.

Or maybe it's because—Forget it. Don't think those thoughts. The virgin and the stud. Only in the movies . . .

Neither of them slept a wink that night. But for all the wrong reasons.

"Steve?"

"What?"

"Are you awake?"

"Now I am."

They both lay in the king-size bed, a wall of pillows between them. Sort of like the Wall of Jericho blanket in *It Happened One Night,* one of her absolutely favorite movies. The great wall of pillows was nothing they had consciously constructed, but Kelly had kind of mounded them around until she felt she was secure in her little corner of the mattress.

"Do you think I'm a big jerk?"

"No. Why?"

"I mean, about the whole . . . virgin thing."

"Oh. That."

He was silent for a long moment, and she waited for his answer.

"No."

"You're sure?"

"Yeah."

"Remember when you said, what's this thing with you and love? I think that's it. I think...I just wanted to be in love."

She rolled over on to her stomach and closed her eyes, determined to forget that Steve Delany was only a few pillows away.

"YOU'RE GOING TO NEED a whole new wardrobe for our honeymoon, and Luis is just the guy to outfit you in a day."

"But I don't have any money."

"It's on me."

She wondered what it was like, to have money you could just toss around like that. But then, Steve probably considered it a career investment, like acting classes or an answering machine.

He called Luis, and the stylist showed up at the bridal suite a little before noon. Kelly spent the next three hours trying on outfit after outfit. Steve sat back in a chair and gave his brutal opinion of each one.

Shirts, skirts, slacks, shorts, sweaters, lounging outfits, evening outfits, bikinis, tank suits...

Kelly drew the line at letting Steve have any say as to the type of underwear she chose. But she did let him see her "honeymoon trousseau."

"I like the black." This comment was made after Luis brought out several negligees and matching peignoirs.

"What is it with men and black?" she asked.

"It works, darling. Don't knock it," Luis remarked, tossing the beautiful nightgown on the huge "to take" pile. The pile of rejects was woefully small, and as Kelly studied all the clothing she would be taking on her honeymoon, she wondered if she'd be spending all her time changing clothes.

"Luis, are all these clothes—are these the types of things women take on cruises?"

"But of course." Luis seemed calm and confident as he swiftly removed price tags and began to fold and arrange the clothing on the king-size bed.

"But I don't want to look like—"

"You won't, *ma petite*. You will be ravishing in these outfits, and Donnatella will be beside herself with rage at the thought of your marrying one of her flings." Luis glanced at Steve, who caught his eye and shook his head.

"But it is true, is it not? She is the dog in the manger, Steve. You know this is so."

He didn't reply, and Kelly sensed he was uncomfortable with their discussion of his past. Again she thought of what a discreet man he was. Until he'd confessed his part in the affair with Donnatella, she'd never even known the two of them were involved.

And she would have. Kelly had an absolute, consuming passion for movie magazines. Many a time, she and Aunt Bette had decided they'd both been born in the wrong era. They belonged to the period that had produced such great magazines as *Photoplay, Silver Screen,* and *Film Fun.*

People paled in comparison.

"Now," Luis said, getting back to business. "We must go shopping for accessories, and then I will come back up with you and help you pack. We will make lists—what goes with what—and you will have no trouble dressing for any occasion. So I will have her for the day, right, Steve?"

Steve nodded his head, deep in thought. Kelly wondered what it was that had captured his attention, but she had no time to worry as Luis clapped his hands and motioned for her to get her purse.

"I'll have her back in time for dinner."

THEY SHOPPED and shopped and shopped. Kelly had never truly understood the expression "Shop 'til you drop," until she'd gone on a spree with Luis.

Scarves. Earrings. Bracelets, necklaces, rings. Bows and bangles and baubles. Handbags, evening bags, beach bags. And shoes—more shoes than she'd owned in her entire life.

Then makeup. All the expensive brands she'd only dreamed about while looking in fashion magazines. For a girl who usually bought one lipstick a season— in a discount drugstore—the collection of makeup she now possessed seemed enormous.

Though they had most of it taken directly to the hotel, they staggered out of the Kahala Mall, weighed down by several packages. Luis had driven his Mercedes, and by the time they found it and loaded their purchases, both of them were wheezing.

"Now, anything else you can think of? You'll be leaving tomorrow morning. There won't be time for any last-minute shopping."

Kelly thought carefully. Her forehead wrinkled in consternation. "Oh, Luis, my suitcase is so shabby—" It seemed that everything about her life before Steve would give Donnatella a clue as to what a complete fake she was.

"Say no more, Steve is having several different styles delivered to the room tonight. You'll choose the one you want and pack it full."

Her mind raced, trying to account for every detail. It seemed everything had been taken care of, except—

"My nerves."

"What?"

"Something for my nerves. I don't know.... Something so I won't feel so nervous all the time. Luis, help me—"

"I know just the thing."

He drove her to Chinatown, and she remembered the lunch she'd shared with Steve. That afternoon seemed so long ago. After parking the car in front of a small store with Oriental lettering on its sign, Luis turned to face her.

"Do you believe in herbs?"

"You mean, do I believe they work?"

"Yes."

"My aunt has a garden full of them. She's been dosing us for as long as I can remember."

"Excellent."

Luis amazed her again once they were inside the tiny store, speaking rapid and fluid Chinese with the proprietor. He was an old man, and Kelly couldn't quite pinpoint his age. Ageless. His eyes were kind, and he had the sort of face that made her suspect he'd seen much in his lifetime.

After the brief discussion with Luis, he retired to the back of the small store to concoct her herbal remedy.

"I'm just going to browse for a second," said Luis. "You let me know if you see anything else you want."

The walls of the store were of some sort of dark wood and the floor was covered with some sort of matting. Though the store seemed dark, the front window was uncurtained and let in a certain amount of bright daylight. But it seemed cooler in here, as if they'd stepped into a different dimension.

The contents on the shelves fascinated her. She couldn't read the labels; many were from Oriental countries. Dragons, monkeys, tigers and snakes graced various labels. Bottles of pills, syrups and cakes of soap were neatly arranged beside boxes of tea bags, bottles of shampoo and jars of cream. Plants grew in a wild disarray in the front window, some of them, herbs she couldn't identify. Every bit of wall space was covered with charts, maps and strange posters.

"Some pearl cream for your skin, and this shampoo is excellent for your color hair...." Luis was talking softly to her as he gathered a few other purchases. She could see how he'd become so very successful—his mind never seemed to rest. Luis was always on to the next thing.

She started when the little Oriental man seemed to appear by her side, a small package in his hand.

"For you," he said, his manner grave. "Just dissolve a pinch in liquid, and you will be calm."

"Thank you very much." She took the package he offered, and suddenly felt confident that her nerves wouldn't have a chance to get the better of her.

"Anything else?" the owner asked. His eyes were so kind, his manner so compassionate, that Kelly wasn't afraid.

"Do you have anything . . . for love?"

"Ahhh." The almond-shaped eyes crinkled when he smiled, and he moved silently to the back of the small shop. Kelly glanced toward the front of the store, where Luis was still browsing. She wasn't embarrassed about his knowing what she'd done, but she wondered at the sudden impulse and where it had come from.

Within a short time, the little man was back, pressing a small vial into her hand.

"Very strong," he said, nodding his head as if she had been wise to ask for this particular herbal combination. "Just a few drops, in coffee, tea or juice."

Kelly nodded her head as Luis came back and set the rest of his choices on the counter.

As the owner was carefully wrapping and bagging their purchases, Kelly reached for the love potion and slipped it into her purse.

Luis appeared not to notice.

But the old man caught her eye and smiled.

SHE LAY IN BED that night, terrified of what was to come.

The only boat she'd ever been on was *Pirates of the Caribbean* at Disneyland. Her only idea of what a cruise entailed came straight off television and movie screens—"The Love Boat." *No,* The Poseidon Adventure.

That's more like it.

Steve shifted in his sleep and rolled over. He'd told her he was a fairly quiet sleeper, but this, the second night they'd shared the huge bed, proved to her that something was bothering him.

Well, take your pick. There's quite a list.

She wasn't sure if Donnatella was going to buy the fact that they were married. Kelly had always thought men were easier to fool than women. Women seemed to have a sixth sense, an intimate radar that prevented them from being fooled emotionally.

She wouldn't know what sort of hot water she was in until she met Donnatella and had a chance to size the woman up for herself. But from everything she and Bette had read over the years, this woman was not going to be a piece of cake to get along with.

Especially if she thought Kelly had something she wanted.

She could hear Steve's even breathing next to her, and for one wild moment she wondered what would happen if she reached out and touched the muscles in his back.

He really was a beautiful man. Granted, his body was part of his business; he got parts in projects because of the way he looked. But if he hadn't been an actor, if he'd been a construction worker or a businessman, he still would have drawn feminine glances wherever he went.

I think you're amazingly attractive....

She couldn't get Steve's comment out of her head. While there were many things she might think about Steve, both good and bad, she knew he wasn't a liar. Even though she'd been totally astounded at the casualness of his affair with Donnatella, he'd been honest with the woman and both of them had known the proverbial score.

And now he was being honest with her.

He'd seemed attracted to her, really attracted to her, until the moment she'd told him she was a virgin. Then he'd backed off so quickly, she hadn't known what had hit her. But then, what man these days wanted a woman with no particular experience? It seemed to shout out the basic fact that no other man had ever found her desirable enough to pursue.

It hadn't been exactly that way. There had been men, and there had been offers. But Kelly, brought up on a steady diet of Clark Gable, Spencer Tracy, John Garfield and Humphrey Bogart, had wanted that little something more.

Adventure, excitement, romance...

Well, now you've got two out of three, and your stomach is killing you....

She thought of the herbal concoction for her nerves, safely in her purse, and decided she would take some. It wouldn't hurt—she needed a restful night's sleep. And this way she could test it before she was trapped aboard *The Aphrodite*.

What had the proprietor said? Dissolve a pinch of the powder in liquid. She slid out of bed as silently as possible, thankful that Steve was asleep, and padded toward the large bathroom in the dark.

HE HADN'T SLEPT a wink.

Now, hearing Kelly slide out of bed and head toward the bathroom, Steve wondered how he was ever going to keep his hands off his little bride for the entire twenty-one days.

Mission impossible.

Even the scripts he was sent didn't come up with plots as wild as this one. If he sat down and pitched this concept to a major studio, no one would buy it.

Truth was truly stranger than fiction.

He squinted his eyes, but could barely make out the soft gleam of light beneath the bathroom door.

This couldn't go on. Another few sleepless nights, lying next to Kelly in bed aboard *The Aphrodite,* and he'd be ready to jump over the side. And Dimi was no fool. Steve knew he wasn't exactly going to present the picture of a contented honeymooner.

He had to think of something, and he had to think of it fast.

What if you just told her you had . . . deep feelings for her? What if you told her you wanted to give this make-believe marriage a real try?

Deep feelings just didn't cut it with a woman who was holding out for the real thing. In a funny kind of way, Kelly reminded him of a young Natalie Wood in *Love with the Proper Stranger,* holding out for banjos and bangles, or whatever the hell she'd said.

She was so heartbreakingly naive, so innocent. It was in her eyes, the way she moved, the things she said.

Donnatella was going to eat her alive. And the woman was just vindictive enough to do it. Because there had been one little thing he'd neglected to tell Kelly, and he didn't dare tell her until they were safely ensconced in their suite of rooms aboard *The Aphrodite.*

Donnatella Marciano hadn't exactly wanted to break off their relationship. He'd been honest with her, honest about what he'd wanted from the weekend, and she had seemed to agree. But this was a woman who was used to getting what she wanted. She reminded him of Dimi in that sense, and he had thought about what a fight between the two of them must be like.

She'd pursued him for quite a while, and whenever they'd met in public, she'd made it quite clear in very unsubtle ways that she'd have no hesitation about starting things up again. Even the thought of Dimi's complete and utter rage didn't have a cooling effect on this woman's libido.

So you're letting Kelly walk into the lion's den, even after you told her you'd protect her. Some hero.

Some husband.

He saw the light click off beneath the bathroom door and quickly closed his eyes. Steve heard Kelly open the bathroom door as quietly as possible, then heard the soft padding of her bare feet on the plush carpeting. The mattress sagged gently as she got back into bed, and he had to resist the urge to reach over and pull the covers around her shoulders, tucking her in.

He sighed into the darkness, and carefully rolled over again, trying to find a comfortable position where his conscience wouldn't bother him.

There was one thing he was sure of: it was going to be a honeymoon to remember.

Something to tell the grandkids.

If he lived that long.

Chapter Six

The Aphrodite redefined luxury, Kelly thought as she gazed out over the Aegean.

The yacht possessed everything one could want, from a bowling alley to three swimming pools. Dimitri had also recently installed a movie theater, complete with an entire authentic multiplex snack bar.

The fixtures in the bathroom were gold, the tub made of Italian marble. The sheets were Porthault, the food prepared by a master French chef who used to run a five-star restaurant outside of Paris. Even the weather had decided to cooperate, as if Dimitri had consulted with the gods.

Kelly had never seen a body of water to compare to the Aegean. The sky had remained blue and cloudless for the first few days, and the islands that dotted the horizon shimmered in the bright sunlight like mystical, mythical kingdoms.

Dimitri's life-style was everything Kelly could have ever imagined. There hadn't been a whim she hadn't been able to indulge in the past seventy-two hours.

And she wasn't enjoying it a bit.

Her fingers tightened on the railing. Donnatella Marciano would arrive tonight, leaving her luxurious Paris apartment and flying to Athens in another of Dimi's private jets. She'd be arriving from Athens by helicopter. Dimitri had informed them of this over brunch this afternoon. He'd smiled indulgently at both of them, taking in their tired faces and the slight circles beneath their eyes.

He'd assumed, of course, that they'd been up all night. They had. But what Dimi didn't know was they'd been awake for all the wrong reasons.

They'd unpacked their bags the same day they'd arrived, and she'd explored the honeymoon suite. A huge bed, large mirrors, a sunken Jacuzzi, a wet bar and, in the bathroom, a sunken tub big enough to give a convention in.

Fresh flowers were everywhere—a riot of color and scent. There had even been the proverbial fruit basket on the main table, filled to the brim with exotic and expensive delicacies. And a box of Belgian chocolates, which she'd promptly confiscated.

Kelly had selected the dresser on the far side of the suite, then unpacked swiftly, trying to coordinate the various outfits according to Luis's instructions. There was nothing she longed for more than a hot bath. Traveling had always made her feel slightly grimy. Traveling in style with Dimitri hadn't given her that exact feeling, but she was exhausted at keeping up the facade that she and Steve were ecstatic honeymooners.

She glanced nervously over her shoulder. Steve was unpacking, as well, and she wondered what he was thinking. His temper had held up remarkably well, all things considered. After all, all she'd really meant to do was slip him a script. How could she have possibly known that they would still be together—very closely together—almost a week later?

After deciding to take up residence in the bathroom for the next few hours, she padded back into the bedroom. She'd kicked off her shoes the minute they'd reached the privacy of their suite.

Steve was sitting on the California king-size bed, staring into space.

She was gathering up a change of clothing when he spoke.

"What would honeymooners do?" he asked.

"Beats me. I mean, besides the obvious."

"Would we be rude enough to leave Dimi to his own devices this evening?"

"I'd vote for that." *Call me a coward, call me a chicken, call me a wimp—it's all true.*

"Maybe Dimi would like some time alone."

"Definitely," she agreed.

"How about this? I'll order up a bottle of champagne, and we'll have dinner in our suite tonight."

"Okay. I'm going to take a bath and a nap. Not at the same time, though."

"That actually sounds pretty good."

When she gave him a suspicious look, he said, "The nap, not the bath."

So the facade was tiring him out, as well. She'd thought with Steve being a professional actor, he wouldn't feel the stress as much as she had.

She'd assumed wrong.

Once inside the bathroom, it had taken her fifteen minutes to explore the massive medicine chest and decide which of the dazzling array of gels and scented bubble baths she was going to select. Deciding on peach-scented bath gel, she'd started the water running and dumped some of the gel in. Shedding her clothing, she'd slid into the tub.

It was the size of a Jacuzzi. She couldn't even reach the golden swan faucets with her toes the way she usually did at home.

The whole bathroom looked as if it belonged on the set of *Cleopatra*.

Her thoughts drifted until the massive tub was completely filled, then she sat up, leaned across and turned off the water. Settling back in billows of scented bubbles, Kelly sighed and finally allowed herself to relax.

The only thing missing is a good book to get my mind off all this.

She'd turned on soft music in the background, then fiddled around with the built-in stereo system until she'd found a rhythm-and-blues station. Aretha Franklin was starting to wail about respect as Kelly sighed and slid beneath the warm water.

If I wanted a book, I'd probably only have to ring for it.

Dimitri also had an extensive library aboard ship. The thought of one of his stern-faced stewards coming into the bathroom with a paperback novel on a silver serving platter made her want to laugh out loud.

Surfacing, she slicked her hair back off her face, then opened her eyes and looked directly at Steve.

And screamed.

And ducked back beneath the bubbles.

Kelly knew she had to surface sooner or later. But she was going to opt for later, with the wild hope that when later occurred, Steve would be out of the bathroom and this whole little incident would soon fade into a mildly embarrassing memory.

How much of her body had he seen?

What was he doing in the bathroom, anyway?

She was trapped on a yacht in the middle of the Aegean with a man she barely knew. Like one of those television "women in jeopardy" movies-of-the-week, the trusting woman with the nice guy who turned out to be psychotic.

Don't panic, he's not crazy—you are.

And besides, this little deal had enabled her to wire the entire amount of money needed for Colleen's operation—and then some—to her Aunt Bette the morning they'd left on this bogus honeymoon. And that counted for a lot in Kelly's book.

She couldn't hold her breath any longer, and surfaced with a splash.

He was still there, standing, looking down at her in the tub. And making strange gestures with his hands.

She frowned, about to open her mouth when he reached over and covered it.

"Quiet," he mouthed.

She almost stopped breathing.

Oh my God. This is it, he's snapped....

As sanity and clarity of thought returned, she could hear a muted clink and rustling coming from the main part of the suite.

"Giggle," he whispered.

Her eyes opened wider in silent appeal.

"As if you were having fun," he whispered, his lips close to her ear.

She was frozen. She couldn't have giggled even if Edward G. Robinson had held a gun to her head.

He reached beneath the water and his hand, with unerring accuracy, found her bottom and pinched it.

She yelped.

He laughed.

He splashed the water around, his attention focused on the suite just beyond the bathroom door. Then, to her absolute and total horror, he began to remove his clothes.

She glared at him.

"Close your eyes, darling," he murmured.

He'd just started to slide off his pants when she did.

She felt him sink into the tub beside her, then grab her foot and start to tickle it.

She whooped, and her eyes flew open.

He laughed—the cad. And looked just as good naked and in the bathtub as she'd known he would.

Then he called out, "Is someone there?"

Silence reigned for just a second, then an accented voice answered, "I am just setting up a little snack tray for the two of you. Mr. Alexandros asked me to bring it down."

"Just a minute," Steve called, then he leapt out of the tub and wrapped a towel around his waist. Kelly got a glimpse of a well-muscled backside—and a tattoo!—before she thought to close her eyes again.

He left the bathroom, and she could hear the two men, laughing and conversing. Then the sound of a door shutting. She knew Steve would be returning to the bathroom, and for a moment thought of locking the door against his entry. But he would only think she was a silly little virgin, so she stifled the urge and tried to look suitably calm as he came back into the room, chilled champagne bottle and two crystal flutes in hand.

"I suppose I should ask you why you thought to get into the tub with me."

"I suppose I have an answer." He deftly uncorked the champagne bottle, then poured them each a glass. Setting the bottle within easy reach of the tub, he offered her one. She took it.

Why, thank you, Mr. Bond. Another surreal adventure with the indomitable Nick Derringer.

"Bernard is Dimitri's private steward. He reports back to him immediately if something isn't up to standards. He's a very observant man."

"How do you know all this?"

"I've done a little snooping of my own concerning Mr. Alexandros."

"Okay. So?"

"So he sends Bernard down to give us this little snack and you're in the bathtub and I'm not? Uh-uh."

"Oh."

"So he'll report back to Dimitri—"

"—That we're having a wonderful time."

She took a sip of champagne and eyed him over the rim of the flute. Thank God for the dense bubbles in the tub. She focused her gaze on the wall behind him, not wanting to pay too much attention to his scantily clad body.

"Do we have to continue having such a wonderful time, or do I get to take my bath in peace?"

He doffed his towel and she closed her eyes.

"Wait a minute—"

"Kelly, you're as jumpy as a flea on a hot stove—"

"My, what a flattering comparison. You're not getting into this tub with me!"

"Just doing my job, ma'am." She could hear the hint of laughter in his voice. "Just think of it like deconditioning. Pavlov's dogs, and all that."

"Oh. So the more I'm around you, the less nervous I'll be?"

"Once you've sat in a tub with me, both of us buck naked, lying around by the pool in our swimsuits should be a breeze."

He had a point, damn him. She couldn't jump every time he touched her or took off a piece of clothing. He was supposed to be the man she loved, the man she'd chosen to marry....

"Oh, get in."

What was it with this man and nakedness? Had living in Hawaii for the past few years and running around without a shirt for the greater part of it fried his brains?

Kelly could hear the water splash, feel it rise as Steve slipped into the tub. At least he had the courtesy to stay a slight distance away from her.

"You're scared of meeting Donnatella, aren't you?"

She opened her eyes and stared at him across what seemed like miles of bubbles. The man could read minds. Or maybe it was just that she was a painfully obvious person. But she was scared—more than scared. She had this weird premonition she was going to be eaten alive.

"Okay. Okay. Yes, I am."

"You're smart to be scared. Donnatella doesn't like being overshadowed by anyone, and she won't hesitate to play dirty. She's going to be jealous that Dimi is so fond of you, so I thought I'd help you."

"How's that?" A bit of suspicion crept into her voice.

"Kelly. You wound me. I promise you, I don't have any ulterior motives in this." There was just a hint of laughter in his voice.

"And I'll bet you have a bridge to sell me."

"No, seriously, as my new bride, there are a few things you should know."

"Like what?"

"Like, I have a birthmark on my left inner thigh. Now, if you want to see it—"

"Just describe it, please."

"It's dark brown and about the size of a dime."

"It doesn't look like anything? Like Cuba or Bora Bora or something?"

"Nope. Just a mark."

"And don't forget your tattoo."

She recalled the glimpse she'd had of his backside.

"Yeah," he said, grinning. "It's a dragon."

"But how come in 'The Nick of Time,' you—"

"Body makeup."

"Oh. Why'd you get it?"

"I was drunk at the time."

It took her a moment to digest that. "Any other bodily markings I should know about?"

"That's it. I've been told I'm a pretty hairy guy."

"I can see that."

"I don't snore."

"I know."

"I'm a sound sleeper."

"But restless."

"Don't tell her I'm restless. She'll get the wrong idea."

"Anything else you've been *told?*"

"I think my body temperature runs a little higher than normal."

"A warm kind of guy."

"You got it."

She took another sip of champagne. It was crazy, it was totally illogical, but she felt safe with this man. He wasn't going to jump her bones, he wasn't going to take advantage of the situation. If the strangest thing they did during their marriage was have conferences in the master bathtub, she could live with it.

As long as the bubbles lasted.

"What else?"

"I'm—I've been *told* I'm a great kisser."

She could feel her face flame. "You've got to be a Leo with that ego."

"August eighth. With Scorpio rising."

She blushed. How could this man hold an innocuous conversation and make her feel as if she'd just called a nine-hundred number off late-night TV?

"And your moon?"

His lips twitched, but she maintained eye contact.

"Capricorn. You?"

"Sun in Sagittarius, moon in Scorpio—don't say it—and Leo rising."

"Hmmm. Interesting. More champagne?"

"Please." After he topped off her glass, she took another sip. "So you're a great kisser. Donnatella knows that, and if she says anything, I'll agree with her."

His hazel eyes were sparkling. "I've also been *told* that I'm a very good lover."

"Not great? I'm surprised."

"Very good, great—feel free to give me any rating you choose. I just thought I might add to your education just a little before Donnatella arrives."

"My *sexual* education."

"We've got to be a little more familiar with each other, or she's going to suspect. I think we have Dimi fooled, but Donnatella won't be as easy."

"So what, precisely, do you propose we do?"

He poured himself another flute of champagne and set the bottle down on the floor by the tub. "First of all, your virtue's safe with me. I've never even been to bed with a virgin before. They're too much trouble."

"Well, excuse me."

"No, what I mean is, they attach too much importance to the act."

"The act? You make it sound like something performed by a Russian circus troupe!"

"You know what I mean."

"I don't think there's anything wrong with attaching a lot of importance to being intimate with another human being."

"I worded it wrong, Kelly. There's nothing wrong with it. You and I just have completely different outlooks on this."

"Meaning, you have a male outlook and mine is female and therefore foolish and emotional."

"I didn't say that. Kelly, don't get all—"

"Emotional! That's what you were going to say, wasn't it?"

"No." He sighed then, and set his flute of champagne down by the side of the tub. "Look, all I'm saying is that Donnatella is sophisticated enough to take one look at you and realize we haven't slept together. I just thought that if we talked about it a little, discussed a few things, you might feel more secure facing her."

"Okay." Kelly took a deep breath and steadied herself, then took another sip of champagne. "You're right. If what you can tell me might make things easier, then I'm all for it. But some of this has to be me, because I'm not as good as you are at playing a part."

"Then tell me."

"Okay. I'm not sophisticated, and I don't think I ever will be. I was a virgin when we met, and a virgin on our wedding night, because I attach a lot of importance to the act, and I didn't want to give that part of myself away to anyone but my husband."

He nodded. "Go on."

"I'm still learning about my own sexuality because we've only been married a few days, and I think it's something that should be kept private between a husband and wife, so if Donnatella pries into anything I consider private, I'll tell her so!"

"Good."

"We met, and I'll try to tell her with a straight face that you were totally overwhelmed by love—"

"Kelly." He took hold of her hand, then took the champagne flute out of her fingers and set it down by the tub. "Kelly, I told you before that I'm attracted to you. But I wouldn't feel right doing anything about that attraction because you really want it all, and I can't give that to you."

"Don't you? Want it all?" she whispered. Somehow, what he'd just said hurt her deeply. Was she so naive that he found her laughable? "Don't you believe in love?"

"No."

She stared at him for a long moment, then swallowed and found her voice. "Then why would Donnatella believe you married me?"

"I'll tell her that I love you. I can act the part."

His confidence infuriated her. "You've never been in love with a woman?"

"No."

What a waste. This man would make any woman a marvelous husband, if he'd only let go of the tight wall she sensed he reined in around his emotions. As she was staring at him, Luis's words came back to her.

You think you know the real Steve Delany, the world thinks it knows who he is. You're both wrong.

Even through the little red warning flares her common sense was sending up in her mind, at that exact moment, Kelly resolved that she was going to solve the mystery that was her husband.

"The water's getting cold," she said.

He turned on the hot water, and Kelly was careful to put more bath gel beneath it. She breathed a sigh of relief as more frothy bubbles burst forth, concealing them both.

"I'll wash your hair," Steve said softly.

"But the soap—the bubbles will disappear."

"I'll use that stuff."

It was body gel, and it would probably make a fine shampoo. She was just about to refuse his offer when a nagging little thought slipped into her mind.

"Did you wash her hair?"

"Yes."

Not understanding the suddenly perverse desire to compete with Donnatella, Kelly handed him the gel and turned her back to him.

He had wonderful hands. They massaged and caressed her scalp, carefully lathering the entire length of her hair until she was almost purring with contentment and leaning into his touch.

She ducked beneath the water and rinsed her hair, then turned to see him watching her.

"Okay. You've got a very nice touch. From what I can tell with my limited experience, that is."

"Don't be ashamed of it, Kelly. It's kind of sweet."

"Yuck."

"No, it is. And I think we can use that angle to explain this marriage. Kind of like, you're so different from the women I'm used to that I was bowled over."

"Yeah, sure."

"You know I'm attracted to you."

She couldn't breathe suddenly; the vast bathroom seemed full of steam and scent and . . . tension. Sexual tension.

She licked suddenly dry lips, and wondered if he could hear the beating of her heart.

"And I'm attracted to you." There was a part of her, a crazy part, she acknowledged freely, that wished he would simply take the entire decision out of her hands. That wished he would reach for her, pull her into his arms, kiss her until she was senseless, then have his wicked way with her.

She had a feeling it was something she would enjoy, on a physical level, very much.

But it would kill something inside her on an emotional level. Without love it wouldn't mean a thing.

"You're turning me on right now," he said, his voice low.

She could feel herself starting to shake, could feel the light hum of excitement beginning to vibrate throughout her body, centering in the soft ache between her thighs.

"Don't play games with me," she whispered.

"I'm not. I'm telling you the truth. Now, you tell me the truth, Kelly. What do you want?"

Emotion seemed to be spilling out of her body, overflowing in the tiny tremors shaking her, in the slight sting of tears. She felt vulnerable and naked and so very, very alive. And she knew it was a feeling that only this man could give her.

"A part of me wants you to just grab me and kiss me and just get it over with. A part of me wants to find out all about it with you." Her voice trembled, and she took a deep breath.

"And?"

"And another part of me would hate myself afterward. Because, even though I know it would probably be wonderful, I don't think I'd feel very good, knowing that—"

"I didn't love you."

She nodded her head.

"It's okay." He touched the side of her face, ran a gentle finger over her cheekbone, and Kelly fought the urge to lean into his touch and simply let physical sensation take over.

But she couldn't.

"It's okay, I'm not going to hurt you. Ever." He drew his hand back, then got up out of the tub. Before she could avert her eyes, she saw without any doubt that she had turned him on. She glanced away then, putting her hands over her face, and heard him enter the shower and turn on the water full blast.

Cold, no doubt.

Now, STARING OUT over the ocean, Kelly knew the moment of truth couldn't be put off much longer. She and Steve had hidden in their suite for the past few days, and only had brunch with Dimi late this morning. He'd expect them to show for this late lunch.

She'd dressed carefully, in one of the outfits Luis had selected for her. A casual outfit, colorful turquoise cotton harem pants and a short-sleeved, cropped top. A brightly colored, braided belt, silver earrings and a simple bracelet had been on the accessory list. She'd discarded the sandals Luis had recommended in favor of plain deck shoes.

Kelly was still getting her sea legs.

"I thought I'd find you out here."

She turned to find Steve walking toward her. He looked fit and tan in jeans, deck shoes and a blue cotton pullover. The wind was strong, and she pulled her hair back with her hands and held it in one hand.

"Have you seen her?"

"No, but I met Dimi on deck. She'll definitely be arriving in time for lunch." He paused. "She's probably already here."

He must have noticed the expression on her face, because he put his arm around her and gave her a gentle hug.

"You can do it, Kel. I have faith in you."

Forcing herself to smile, she walked with him toward the dining area.

DONNATELLA MARCIANO was everything Kelly had thought she would be. On seeing the older woman, she immediately wished she'd worn the sandals, much more makeup, some perfume and had possessed the foresight to pull her hair up into a sophisticated style.

Oh, where was Luis when she needed him!

Instead, she let Steve pull out her chair and seat her, then she smiled at the dark-haired woman as Dimitri introduced them. She wondered at the man's motives, at the games he seemed to like to play among all his friends. What satisfaction could he be getting out of this bizarre gathering? Was this the idea of a good time among the rich and famous?

She tried not to stare at Donnatella as the meal was being served. The woman was incredibly striking, with dark hair scraped off her face in a style only the most attractive women can wear, light olive skin and black, liquid eyes. She had high cheekbones, and was wearing pure red lipstick on her full, expressive mouth.

The exquisitely styled black halter dress looked like something Kelly had seen in Italian *Vogue* three months ago. Solid gold hoops adorned her ears, and an enormous diamond pendant hung between her generous breasts. Kelly remembered the article Bette had pointed out to her about that particular pendant—how many carats it was, how much it had cost.

Her black leather sandals had to cost the earth, and Kelly knew Donnatella was not a deck shoe kind of gal.

But precisely what Donnatella Marciano was eluded Kelly.

One of the world's top sopranos, she sang classic opera all over the world. But she was just as renowned for her fiery love affairs with famous men. Her affair with Dimitri had brought both of them a sort of notoriety in the jet-setting world.

After Dimitri had lost his third wife, Tina, he'd vowed he would never marry again. He'd been through a number of women when he met Donnatella, and according to what Kelly and Bette had read in the *National Star,* it had been lust at first sight. Donnatella had led Dimi on a merry chase, then had shocked the world when she turned down his proposal.

They had been together for almost a decade, and their tempestuous union showed no signs of getting any less difficult. But, as both of them seemed to genuinely like things the way they were, Kelly supposed they were happy.

She tried to appear as calm as possible while the courses were served. Normally, it was a lunch she would have enjoyed: fried calamari, pasta with a spicy tomato-based sauce, a fresh salad, French bread and a good red wine. Dimitri ruled over meals on his yacht like a king in the midst of his small, beloved kingdom, and today was no exception.

"So, we haven't seen you two in a couple of days, eh?" he said, breaking off a piece of bread and placing it on his plate. "Has everything been satisfactory?"

Kelly sensed there was a double meaning to his words, and she turned to Steve, deciding to let him answer for both of them.

"More than satisfactory."

"I never thought you would marry." This was from Donnatella, and Kelly's stomach clenched as she saw those intelligent dark eyes hone in on Steve.

This woman wouldn't miss much.

"Neither did I," Steve replied easily. He gave Kelly a slow, intimate grin, and she glanced away, flustered. It unnerved her, playing a part this way. She wished she'd stayed in her acting class longer than a year.

"Oh, I brought you this from Paris. A friend of mine has a subscription." Donnatella reached down into an enormous carryall, pulled out a tabloid paper and tossed it onto the table next to Kelly. "They certainly got this issue out fast enough, don't you think?"

Kelly would remember the strange sensation for the rest of her life. She, who had always read the tabloids in line at the supermarket and then sheepishly paid for them, found herself looking at a picture of herself and Steve in an intimate embrace.

It took her a moment to place the photo, and she realized it was that third kiss. She had a slightly dazed expression on her face. The photo had been blown up, and took up the entire cover.

The headline screamed Derringer Takes The Plunge And Marries Woman Of Mystery!

Woman of Mystery...I like that.

"Thank you," she said softly, trying to make some sort of contact with Donnatella. She sensed that this was a woman who thought of all other women as adversaries. Perhaps she was close to her mother or sister, but most women would not be in the running for best friend.

Donnatella smiled, but the smile didn't reach her eyes. "I thought it was incredibly tacky. I mean, having your wedding photos on the front of a rag like that! Steve, how could you? Unless, of course, you needed the money. A friend of mine mentioned to me that he'd heard you actually *sold* the pictures...."

Kelly didn't hear the rest. She didn't need to. Donnatella reminded her of a sleek, black cat that played with its prey before eating it. And enjoyed frightening the little mouse even more than biting its head off.

She didn't know what to say, and again glanced at Steve. His arm came around her bare shoulders and she reacted to his touch before she could help herself. Donnatella didn't miss much, and her dark eyes narrowed.

The woman was not a happy camper.

"Damn right I did," Steve replied. "Those bloodsuckers have made millions off the imaginary stories they've printed about me. Donna, you know as well as I do that they would have found a way to crash my wedding. This way, at least there was some semblance of control, no one got hurt and I made a hefty amount of money."

"I didn't realize you were in need of a little cash, darling."

Bitch. Saying it in front of Dimitri, and before Steve's negotiated his contract....

She couldn't stand still for it. Kelly smiled brightly, reached for the large bowl of pasta and said, "Oh, but he's not. He gave the entire check to charity. I can't remember which one, but it's an organization that helps needy families cover their medical expenses."

The frosty, haughty look Donnatella bestowed on Kelly told her she'd made an enemy. In *The World According to Donnatella,* there was only room for one female at the table to have a mouth, an opinion or make her presence known.

"How generous of you," Donnatella said, almost whispering the words. At that instant, Kelly knew who the woman reminded her of. Malefecent, in Walt Disney's animated cartoon, *Sleeping Beauty.* Kelly covertly glanced around, almost expecting to see a beady-neyed raven swoop down and settle on the woman's shoulders.

They all busied themselves with eating for the next few minutes, and Kelly wondered if she was the only one at the table who sensed the tension in the air.

She relaxed when she felt Steve gently touching her hair, playing with a few of the tendrils in the way a lover might.

But we're not lovers, and never will be....

The thought depressed her, and she concentrated on her pasta, missing the petulant look Donnatella shot at Steve.

Dimitri insisted on taking meals outside when the weather was good, and today was no exception. The long table was situated under a canvas awning, with views of the ocean shimmering brightly in the noonday sun all around them. The wind had died down to a gentle breeze, and the whole atmosphere would have actually been quite pleasant if it hadn't been for the presence of one woman.

"I found it very hard to believe, Steve, that when you finally married you chose a woman none of us knew." Donnatella was stabbing at her pasta with delicate little strokes, and Kelly had to consciously remind herself not to stare at the woman. Looking at Donnatella was akin to studying a cobra in a reptile house. A fascinating revulsion.

"What's so hard to understand?" Steve said, and Kelly admired the way he lobbed the question back to the diva, putting her on the spot.

"Well, I thought you would have married someone like...an actress, for instance, or a beautiful model...."

Kelly caught the intended slur, and forced herself not to react.

"Kelly's a screenwriter, a woman with brains. But that's not what attracted me to her." Steve gently stroked her cheekbone with one of his knuckles, and Kelly shivered. It was partly in reaction to his touch, but also because she hadn't missed the narrowing of Donnatella's catlike eyes.

The woman was trouble.

"And what did?" Donnatella asked sweetly.

"I don't know…it's kind of hard to explain. It just kind of hit, like *boom,* right in the old solar plexus. The only thing I knew the moment I met her was that I couldn't let her go."

How true. Funny how Steve tells the truth but twists it to his own advantage, Kelly thought. Then she stopped thinking as Steve gently took her chin in his hand, turned her face to his and kissed her.

The man could kiss in such a way that he obliterated all rational thought as soon as their lips touched. She put her palms on his shoulders to steady herself and stop that peculiar inner trembling. He stroked her bare shoulder with his other hand. A lover's touch.

Donnatella spoke up, determined to break the intimate moment.

"But—and you'll pardon me saying this, Kelly—she's such a *baby,* Steve. The women you usually go out with aren't as…oh, how should I say it—"

"Innocent, Donna? That was part of the attraction."

Kelly saw the slight color flood the older woman's cheekbones, and she laid a restraining hand on Steve's arm. There was no use in getting Donnatella riled up on the first day they were all together. After all, they had seventeen glorious, fun-filled days to go.

"Innocent, eh?" Donnatella said, glancing straight at Kelly. "So you played the oldest game in the world, didn't you? You held out and made him marry you." The tone of voice was playful. Teasing. But there were dark, nasty undercurrents here.

"Well, you're right. I held out. But the marriage was his idea, not mine."

Steve, in the midst of sipping his wine, choked on the liquid, then started laughing.

"What a peculiar little creature you are."

Kelly bit her tongue, determined not to react. But Steve sobered instantly at the slur.

"Donna, I won't have you talking to my wife that way."

Kelly glanced over at her husband. He was eyeing Donna now, and Kelly was reminded of two animals, staring off, each waiting for the other to roll over on its belly and give the other dominance.

"Oh, Steve, don't go all macho on me! I was simply having a little fun! Wasn't I, Kelly?"

She turned her attention back to the woman across from her, and found her voice.

"I'm sure you didn't mean for it to be an offensive remark, but I guess I'm just not as—*experienced* as you are. So I'm sure you won't mind making things comfortable for me while I get the hang of all this teasing." She smiled then, her sunniest smile, and was rewarded by the quick flash of puzzlement she sensed from Donnatella.

She thinks I'm a simpleton. That's okay—for now.

The rest of the meal seemed interminable. Fresh fruit and cheese was brought out for dessert. Kelly had adored this particular dessert only a day ago; the pears were so sweet and ripe you could eat them with a spoon. But today she had no appetite. As soon as she could, she excused herself and walked back to the suite she shared with Steve.

Throwing herself onto their large bed, she gazed up at the ceiling and thought of the days ahead, stretching out endlessly before her. Now that she'd met Donnatella and seen the woman in action, Kelly didn't want to think about what nasty little tricks the woman had in store for her.

Chapter Seven

"She's on to us. I just know it."

"Kel, don't go all panicky on me. We've got fourteen days to go, and I don't think she suspects a thing. Look at how much time we've been spending in this room. What can she suspect when she never sees us?"

The two of them were lying in bed, relaxing after a long day of playing happily marrieds.

It hadn't been all that hard to pretend.

They'd spent the morning in their suite, ordering breakfast in. Then, after lunch, they'd lazed by the large outdoor pool. Once Donnatella joined them, by unspoken mutual consent they'd avoided her, moving into the water, swimming, playing and splashing each other.

And he'd kissed her.

This man was to kissing what Dom Pérignon was to champagne, beluga was to caviar and Dimitri was to money.

It's not fair, Kelly thought as she covertly studied him. He even looked cute in glasses. The public didn't know Nick Derringer was farsighted, because Steve wore contacts when he worked. At night, relaxing in the privacy of their suite, he wore glasses when he read. They were perched down low on his nose as he studied the script Dimi was planning to film. He looked like every girl's fantasy of what a college professor should be.

She was finding out a lot about Steve Delany. Unlike "Daring Derringer," as the press had labeled him, Steve really seemed to like their quiet nights in. Their quiet, enforced nights in, she amended silently.

She was reviewing some hastily scribbled notes about the scenes and structure of her next writing project, another screenplay.

Anything to keep her mind off... him.

It was harder than she'd thought, keeping her husband out of her thoughts. And it didn't help that the screenplay was a romantic comedy, her absolutely favorite genre. And that its story line seemed to be running parallel to her experiences with Steve.

She'd toyed with the idea of titling it, *Let's Make a Deal.*

Even burying herself in her work, she couldn't get her mind off him.

The him in question was totally engrossed in the project that had gotten both of them into this mess in the first place. From what she'd learned in her acting class, she couldn't fault his preparation. His copy of the script was riddled with notes as he questioned his character's motivation, broke the screenplay down into workable beats and figured out unique ways to express his character visually on screen.

He was a worker, and that was a quality she understood.

Earlier this evening, Dimi had insisted on gathering everyone together in his movie theater to see several of his friend's latest films. Kelly had gotten quite a kick out of seeing major studio projects before they were officially released. She guessed it was a normal occurrence to Steve, what with all the premieres he attended.

Donnatella had kept her eagle eye on both of them, but Kelly had simply snuggled closer to Steve and enjoyed her popcorn.

You enjoyed it a little too much, if you ask me, her conscience nagged her.

So, who asked you? she replied.

She couldn't keep her eyes off him. How could he lie in bed next to her, a pillar of masculine calm, when she was a virginal volcano vibrating with raging hormones? Kelly had always thought she'd wait for true love to appear on the horizon. Now, for the first time in her life, she understood why a woman would throw caution to the winds and simply let the good times roll.

Steve Delany was quite an enticement. He looked too good, stretched out on top of the duvet, with only his pajama bottoms on.

They'd spent their first night in the suite negotiating what kind of clothing they would both wear to bed. Steve had blithely informed her that he was used to parading around in the altogether, and Kelly had just as blithely replied that he was going to have to cover it up around her.

She had been totally dismayed to see that Luis had somehow snuck her favorite, frayed nightshirts out of her suitcase and replaced them with enough erotic lingerie to stock a branch of Victoria's Secret.

They'd compromised. Steve had been thoughtful enough to pack several pairs of men's pajamas. He'd wear the bottoms, while she laid claim to the tops. He was a tall man, so his tops came halfway down her thighs, and were baggy enough on her slender frame so they couldn't possibly be misconstrued as naughty nightwear.

Just like Rock Hudson and Doris Day, she'd thought, the first night she and Steve had retired to bed together. And then she'd remembered that entire wonderful series of movies, how Doris and Rock had fought, bickered, argued—and ended up falling in love.

Wake up, Kelly. This is not a movie. This is your life.

She stared at the notes in front of her, determined not to look at her husband again for at least another five minutes.

Maybe three.

Their suite was so utterly quiet that they both heard the slight, scratching noise at the same time.

She glanced over at Steve. He was frowning, then met her gaze and put a finger to his lips. Comprehension seemed to dawn in his expression as he set his script down on his nightstand. He took her pages out of her hands and put them on top of his script.

She didn't say a word when he turned off both bedside lamps and pulled her beneath the covers with him.

"It's Donnatella," he whispered, his mouth close to her ear. Too close. It felt too good.

"What!" She was shocked at the thought of the lengths this woman would go to. What was it with her, that she had to have the attention of every good-looking man on the yacht. How selfish could the woman be?

"I think she's picking the lock...."

"Oh, come on—"

"Kiss me...."

It wasn't a request she wanted to refuse.

And he was a good kisser. Whoever had told him that had been right. They'd kissed over lunch, by the pool, walking on the deck, in Dimi's movie theater, over dinner, in the library, in Dimi's salon over conversation... The list was endless. Actually, they'd kissed in every possible location on Dimitri's yacht.

But not in bed.

It was different, somehow. You could get closer. Kiss deeper. She felt his hands come down and cup her bottom, the thin silk of her panties offering absolutely no barrier to the warmth and heat of his touch. This kiss was more insistent, more passionate, filled with masculine determination and need.

A prelude to lovemaking.

She didn't have time to think, she could only feel. Her feelings made any response but a total, unthinking one impossible. It shocked her, how rational thought melted away in the face of a physical, sensual attraction as potent as this one.

She kissed him back, encouraged him on, holding on to his shoulders, then clenching her fingers in his hair. Every move she made, every gesture or motion simply served the need to get closer, closer....

She didn't know when she was suddenly aware of another person in the room, but her immediate tension communicated itself wordlessly to Steve. He sat up in bed, throwing the comforter off both of them, and glanced toward the main door of their suite.

"What the hell are you doing in here?"

The bedside lamp clicked on, and Kelly took a quick glimpse.

Donnatella was standing at the foot of their bed, her mouth open in shock.

Steve, kneeling on the mattress, all masculine outrage and disgust. And clearly aroused through the thin cotton of his pajama bottoms.

Kelly, sitting up in the middle of their bed, hair disheveled, glancing down and realizing her top two buttons had come unbuttoned and her breasts were clearly visible.

When did that happen?

Then, embarrassed to the core, she groaned, grabbed a handful of covers and burrowed into the bed. Even with her head beneath a pillow, she could hear the argument that raged around her quite clearly.

"Answer me!"

"Oh, Steve, come on! You marry this little nobody out of the blue, and expect me to believe that she keeps you happy? I know you, darling, what you like, what you need. And I know there's something about this whole thing that doesn't smell right!"

"Get the hell out of this room and don't ever come back!"

"Why don't you come into my bed and let me show you the difference between a little girl and a woman—"

"*Out!*"

From the scuffling noises, Kelly guessed Steve was bodily throwing Donnatella out. The tension of the past few days, tonight's humiliation and Donnatella's stinging, bitter words all combined to overwhelm her.

She burst into tears.

Steve was back within the minute. Her hands were cupped tightly over her face, so she didn't see him. She simply felt his weight depressing one side of the mattress, then his strong arms enfolding her. Then they were lying in bed together, tightly entwined, but there was nothing remotely sexual about this particular experience.

"She's so...so *horrible*," Kelly choked out.

"I know, I know. Shhh." He kissed her forehead, kissed her nose, hugged her tightly. "I'll talk to Dimi tomorrow. We can leave—"

"No! No, you won't get the part—"

"I don't want it anymore. Not if it's going to hurt you."

She burrowed closer, and he held her until she fell asleep.

HE HELD HER all through the night.

Neither of them noticed they hadn't constructed the wall of pillows that night. Or that they never used it again.

Steve lay in the king-size bed, his arms around Kelly as he stared at the ceiling.

When did it suddenly become real?

The kiss tonight had started out as a simple ploy to fool Donnatella. But it had escalated into something much more than that.

Kelly was driving him crazy. It seemed that every few days, his feelings toward her took another turn.

First, she'd been the fresh-faced kid who'd climbed over the balcony. Then, she'd metamorphosed into Jessica Rabbit. He'd had no trouble deciding on having a brief affair with her, but she'd done another quick change and transformed herself into a woman who made him laugh and look at the ridiculousness in life.

He genuinely liked her.

He genuinely wanted to go to bed with her.

Then, suddenly—*poof!*—she'd become a vestal virgin, and as untouchable as the moon.

I'm losing my mind.

He could presumably have his pick of eighty-seven percent of America's women, and he wanted the craziest redhead since Lucille Ball.

Go figure.

By the time this honeymoon's over, I'll have taken so many cold showers, I'll be able to audition for the California Raisins.

He glanced over and saw Kelly lying peacefully beside him, sleeping like a baby. As if she didn't have a care in the world.

Sighing, he got up. Within minutes, the stillness of a night at sea was broken by the sound of running water.

DIMITRI WAS FURIOUS, and demanded that Donnatella offer Kelly a full-scale apology at breakfast the following morning.

Donnatella apologized, but Kelly knew the Italian beauty was furious with her, and angry with Steve because he had protected her.

And Kelly, after vetoing Steve's private suggestion that they leave, took a long walk with Dimitri that afternoon and tried to figure out Donnatella.

"Why does she hate me so much?" she asked. They were out walking on the upper deck, gentle breezes playing with her hair. Dimitri strode ahead of her, walking so briskly that she had to practically jog-walk to keep up with him.

"You have everything she wants," Dimi replied.

"She wants Steve?"

"She's wanted him for a long time."

Kelly thought for a moment about her next question, then asked it anyway. "And that doesn't bother you?"

"Not much bothers me anymore."

A cryptic answer, and one she wasn't satisfied with. "Why?"

"Ever since Tina, I haven't had much of a heart."

Christina Andropolis, Dimitri's third wife. He'd been forty-five when they'd married, she'd been nineteen. Born into a peasant's existence, Tina had been walking with her little brother in a small Greek village when Dimitri had first laid eyes on her. She'd possessed a truly breathtaking beauty, and he'd wanted to possess her the moment he'd laid eyes on her.

Their courtship had amused the press to no end—this big, burly, international businessman sitting down to dinner with a peasant family of twelve, none of whom could read or write.

But Dimitri had been determined. He'd slowly won over Tina's father, then her mother and finally her grandmother. When he'd asked all three permission to marry their beloved child, it had been granted.

Dimitri had adored his young bride. Tina had remained the same woman she'd always been—earthy, unpretentious and kind. Exactly nine months after their wedding day, she'd presented him with his fifth child and their first, a baby boy.

Dimitri's joy had known no bounds.

They named him Stefanos, and for a short while the gods had smiled on Dimitri and his bride.

Tina had died in a plane crash along with their infant son. And the world had mourned with Dimitri at his unspeakable loss.

He'd gone on a publicly recorded rampage of self-destruction, until he'd finally accepted his beloved family was gone forever.

Kelly remembered. She and her Aunt Bette had read every article that had come out about the Greek millionaire, and had suffered for him. Bette had been so upset, she'd carefully clipped each article out and made a scrapbook. Something about Dimitri's story had moved her.

"All the money in the world," Bette had said, "and he can't bring back his beautiful wife and that darlin' baby boy. You remember this, Kelly, when you think money can bring you happiness, 'cause it can't."

Now, walking beside this man, Kelly began to think she knew him a little better. And she understood, in a funny kind of way, why Dimitri strove to keep himself constantly entertained. And constantly around people.

His evenings alone had to be hellish. There was never any escape from your memories.

And she felt a sudden rush of shame, thinking Donnatella Marciano was any sort of problem.

Donnatella was small potatoes.

"I'm sorry about the whole thing last night. I shouldn't have made such a fuss—"

"No." Dimitri silenced her with a single word. "The bedroom is a sacred place, and should remain private. She had no right to do what she did, and that is why I demanded an apology from her."

"Thank you."

They walked in silence for a time, then Dimitri said, "She doesn't really know what to do with you, Kelly. You're very different from the sort of women she knows. And it frustrates her, that she cannot understand how you and Steve have decided to make a marriage."

Kelly remained silent, sensing he had more to say.

"I will be honest with you and admit that, at first, I did not understand your marriage, either. I've known Steve for a number of years. He worked with a friend of mine in a few Italian films, and we met at that time. I've always thought he was a tremendously talented actor, but misunderstood and miscast."

"I agree."

"He had a reputation back then, of being something of a—I'm not sure how to say this without offending you."

"It's all right. I know about his past."

"But that is all changed now, eh?"

"Yep."

He laughed at that, and they continued walking. The Aegean was a brilliant blue today, the sky clear and calm, almost cloudless. The weather was hot, and it felt good to walk briskly.

"I didn't think he would ever settle down."

Oh, Dimi, if you only knew.

"But love has a way of striking when we least expect it. And there is a saying that the reformed rake makes the best husband."

"He's going to make a wonderful husband," she said softly.

Someday. To someone.

LATER, SHE AND STEVE walked on the moonlit deck.

She took a deep breath. "We fooled him. He believes this marriage is a love match. He said as much while we were walking this afternoon."

"It's because of you." She could see his hesitation, then he said, "Everything that's been good about this whole plan has come from you. You have this ability to bring out the best in people."

She held her breath, sensing that this was as close to a declaration of affection as she was ever going to get from this man.

"You certainly bring out the best in me."

She thought he was going to kiss her, but instead he put his arm around her and they walked slowly back to their honeymoon suite.

LYING NEXT TO HER in bed each night was as close to torture as Steve ever wanted to come.

If you told her you loved her as much as you're capable of loving...

He punched his pillow and rolled over. He couldn't remember the last time he'd had a decent night's sleep.

Tonight, while they'd been walking on deck, he'd wanted to ask her to marry him.

But we are married.

He wanted a marriage of *in*convenience.

For real.

Forever.

But his past kept intruding.

There were times, late at night, when he felt that the facade he'd created for the public threatened to choke him. A loving mother and father, three supportive siblings, a large house in a small town in Oregon, an idyllic upbringing...

All of it was false. The only way he'd been able to get away with it was because he'd asked the press not to go after his family. They were private people, he'd said. He wished to respect that privacy, and not let his career infringe on any of them.

The press had liked him from the moment he'd winked at the public from their television sets. But they'd exacted a price, and he'd been more than willing to pay it.

In return, he'd promised, my life shall be yours—an open book.

I won't hide anything from you. I'll even let you put my wedding pictures on the front page. I'll give interviews, I'll pay my public dues, I'll never be too busy to sign an autograph or chat for a minute. . . .

His fictional family was private, all right.

His actual family was lost. All of them. He'd been eight years old when his brother Billy had died. Nothing much had seemed to matter for a long time after that.

The career had been a way of escaping, of keeping busy and of earning a substantial buck. The various women had been a way of getting close, but not too close. He'd never wanted to get close to any of them because he'd never wanted to put himself in a position where he could lose someone else he loved.

But he needed that little bit of human contact in order to convince himself he was still alive, and could still feel something besides the emotions he engendered for the camera.

Then Kelly'd climbed over to his balcony and blown into his life with the force of an emotional tornado. He'd understood instinctively, on a totally emotional level, what it meant to take care of a younger sibling. He'd wanted to give her that chance.

And at the time, he'd wanted the part. He'd wanted to prove to himself that he was capable of running even faster and harder, because sometimes the memories had a way of sneaking up on him and overwhelming him.

He glanced over at Kelly. She was sprawled on her side of the mattress on her stomach, sleeping with her mouth open. She was crazy, she was emotional, but he wasn't frightened of her because she was exactly who she was and always laid all her cards on the table.

He knew she was falling in love with him. She didn't even have the guile to hide the expression in her eyes, or the way she always tried to sneak looks at him. Steve didn't make this assessment out of some unbridled ego. As an actor, he'd been trained to observe. And Kelly was a wonderful subject. So open.

He marveled at that, because from what he knew about her life, she'd had it tough.

She's braver than you are, she comes out swinging and ready to take on the world. She still believes in miracles, and she wants your love....

He wanted to give it to her. But old habits were hard to break. He'd traveled on his own for so long, he wasn't used to having anyone along for the ride. But looking at the little redhead lying next to him in bed, he knew he'd think up something else to keep her by his side until he managed to figure out what to do with her.

Steve closed his eyes and breathed deeply, evenly, willing sleep to come and claim him. Wanting an end to the thoughts racing around in his mind.

The only thing he knew, as he began to drift off, was that he couldn't let her go.

HE FOUND HER on an upper deck the following morning. She was sitting cross-legged in front of a tiny brass incense burner. Her eyes were closed, her face composed, as the thin plumes of white smoke rose up into the brilliant blue sky and vanished.

He waited until she opened her eyes before approaching her.

"Hey."

"Hi." She patted the deck next to her, so he sat.

"Buddhists always burn incense when someone of great importance dies. It's like sending the smoke up to heaven for them." She smiled.

"My mom would've been forty today. I always burn a little incense for her. I like to think that she can see it."

She'd told him her mother had died, but she hadn't said anything about how young she was when Kelly had been born. Doing a quick calculation in his head, Steve realized she would have given birth to Kelly when she was seventeen.

He put his arm around her.

"She'd be so happy for me, being back in Greece, seeing all the islands. I think that's what she gave me that I treasure most; that desire to see things."

She laid her head against his shoulder, and he was overcome by the simple trust she placed in him, the way she believed in him.

He thought of the memories she had of her mother, and for a moment, envied her.

"Did you tell her about Colleen?"

"How'd you know I talk to her?"

He took a breath. "I had a brother. Billy died when he was five."

"How old were you?"

"Eight."

"I didn't know—"

"I don't like to talk about it. It's not something I wanted to share with the public."

He watched her lean forward and put another of the small cones of incense on the tiny burner, then strike a match and ignite it. Thin plumes of scented smoke rose into the air as she leaned back into the circle of his arms.

"Then that's for Billy."

Later, when she asked him, he would tell her that was the exact moment he'd realized how much he loved her and wanted her in his life forever. The final inner wall of the shell he'd built around himself shattered, leaving raw emotion beneath. But risking that love by declaring it to Kelly...

He couldn't. Not yet. Maybe not ever.

Chapter Eight

Gazing out over the Aegean as the sun rose, Kelly wondered if she and Steve would have become as close if they hadn't had as formidable an opponent as Donnatella.

It was something to think about. Lately, Kelly couldn't seem to fathom what was going on in Steve's mind. She'd catch him looking at her in the strangest ways. At times she wondered if he regretted the whole deception.

Kelly sighed, then propped her chin in her hands. She wanted Steve to love her, but she could have been wishing for the moon for all the good it was going to do her.

Oh, but she could wish. And dream.

She was good at that.

A month ago she was in her small Valley apartment plugging away at her screenplay and concocting a plan to help Colleen. Since then, she'd been to Hawaii on a desperate mission, and here she was on a yacht in the middle of the Aegean.

Miracles did happen, she thought. *Every single day.*

And tomorrow—thanks to her dream and the determination to make it happen—Colleen would have her surgery.

Kelly wished, with all her heart, that she could have been with her sister. But Bette had reassured her that everything was going to be fine, she was holding down the fort in Los Angeles and there was no need for Kelly to interrupt her honeymoon.

Oh, but I wish...

Her reverie was interrupted by the sound of helicopter rotary blades, and she looked up at the gloriously clear sky to see a sleek black machine heading straight for the yacht's helipad.

Strange, she thought. Dimi hadn't mentioned anything about guests.

She saw him walking toward her and waved. "Guests?" she called out over the noise of the helicopter.

"No." The dark, deeply olive eyes lit up with emotion as he grinned. "Arrangements have been made for you to go to Athens, then fly to Los Angeles to spend time with your sister. How soon can you leave?"

She stared at him, speechless. It was too much, it was all she'd ever wanted, it was...perfect.

"Dimi!" Without thinking, she threw herself into his arms and hugged him fiercely.

"Family is family," he said.

"How can I ever thank you for this?" she whispered.

"Don't thank me. Thank your husband. He is the one who arranged all of this."

SHE WAS DEEPLY TOUCHED by the fact that Steve insisted on coming with her.

"You're going to need someone else there with you," he'd said as he'd helped her throw things into her suitcase. She'd been so delirious with happiness she hadn't really paid attention to what she was packing.

Someone to lean on. It was a foreign concept, and one she found she liked very much. If he hadn't suggested going along, she never would have voiced the thought. He'd already done enough for her for one lifetime.

"I'd like that."

Now, as she and Steve entered the teaching hospital at UCLA, she was glad he'd come with her.

Bette was sitting by Colleen's bed when they entered the private room. Kelly felt Steve's slight hesitation at barging into this intimate scene, but she kept hold of his hand and made sure he stepped inside.

She'd asked Bette to keep her arrival secret, and the expression on Colleen's face was worth every single mile she'd traveled in the past day.

"Kelly!"

She looked lost in the white hospital bed, lost among the masses of flowers. Her blond hair was tied back in a ponytail, and Kelly focused on her sister's gentle green eyes and saw what she'd wanted to see for such a very long time.

Hope. And if Colleen would allow herself to hope, anything was possible.

Kelly let go of Steve's hand and went to her sister.

"Nice flowers," she said, sitting down on the seat closest to the head of the bed.

"Dimitri sent me a bouquet! The orchids, over there. And Steve did, too." Colleen glanced shyly at her brother-in-law. "Thank you."

"No problem." He was standing by the door, and it seemed to Kelly he was trying to appear as unobtrusive as possible. She heard a soft squeal as a nurse caught sight of him, then saw Steve frown, step all the way inside the room and close the door.

"Y'all talk quick now. She's due in surgery in less than an hour," Bette said quietly. "I'm goin' to go get a cup of coffee, then I'll be right back up—"

"I can get it," Steve offered.

"What, and have half the student nurses traipsing through just to get a look? Uh-uh, honey. You stay right here." And with that, Bette slipped through the door, closing it tightly behind her.

"I'm something of a nuisance, I suppose," Steve muttered to no one in particular.

"No!" Colleen said. "No. I think you're just what Kelly has always wanted."

"Colleen!"

"Remember those letters we wrote that Christmas? When Sharon Donavan told me Santa Claus didn't exist?" She turned her attention to Steve, her thin face flushed and animated. "I was only six, and Kelly was so mad! I'd never seen her so mad. Anyway, she told me we were both going to write letters to Santa, and ask for what we wanted most in the entire world."

"And?" Steve asked, approaching the bed.

Kelly shot him a look. He seemed a lot more interested in the information in this particular story than it would normally warrant.

"She wanted to fall madly and desperately in love with a wonderful man and live happily ever after." Colleen smiled up at Steve. "Kelly's very romantic, but you know that."

"I sure do."

"And do you remember what I wished for?"

Kelly nodded, unable to speak. She'd tucked her sister into bed, listened to her excited chattering and all the while she'd burned to see that note. Whatever Colleen had asked for, she'd move heaven and earth to make sure old Santa delivered.

Bette had been sitting on the couch, staring at the lights on the small tree.

"Don't read it, darlin'." Her mouth had trembled. "There's nothin' you can do."

Of course, then she had to.

Please, Santa, can you fix my heart . . . ?

Kelly couldn't stop the tears that rushed to her eyes at the memory, and bowed her head.

"But don't you see, Kelly, we both got our wishes!"

"Yeah, only five years later." She laughed and reached for a tissue on the bedside stand.

"But we got them. And so maybe it wasn't Saint Nick, but it was still a Nick." She beamed at them. "Nick Derringer."

DR. BENEDICT HAD COME out with good news. Surgery had progressed smoothly, without a single hitch. Colleen was as good as new. Better.

In ten days she'd go home and begin an entirely new life.

Late tomorrow, he and Kelly would return to *The Aphrodite,* and in less than a week their honeymoon would be over.

What then?

He didn't know.

The only thing he could think of was to make up another diversion, keep her with him a little longer, play for some time.

And then what will you pull out of your sleeve?

He wasn't used to being close to people. Not the way Kelly had wormed her way into his heart. He couldn't quite figure out what she'd done. He was used to all the feminine trickery; he'd seen so much of it living in Los Angeles and then Honolulu.

She hadn't tricked him. She'd merely fallen in love with him. The whole situation was deadly, playing with his emotions and twisting his gut so he didn't know what he was going to do.

He'd had no compunctions about fooling the public. But fooling Kelly was something altogether different.

He took a swallow of Scotch. Both Kelly and Bette had been exhausted, and instead of their returning to their respective homes and starting dinner, he'd booked a suite at the Westwood Marquis and called up room service. They'd barely pecked at their food, then taken quick showers and tumbled into bed.

Now he stood out alone on a balcony, looking out over Westwood Village, and wondering what he was going to do.

Keep her with you, a little voice inside him nagged.

For what? he countered. *You have nothing to offer her.*

He downed the rest of the liquor in another swallow, and set the glass down on a nearby table. Leaning against the balcony railing, he wondered at all the tiny steps, the decisions that had led him to this particular place in time.

He hadn't played fair. He'd manipulated the facts so that she'd stay with him. Ever since their night at The White Orchid, he'd wanted her. Then, as he'd gotten to know her, it had started to become something much deeper. He was reluctant to call it love; he only knew he didn't want her to walk away.

He'd tricked her and he hadn't played fair, but the one thing he'd decided early on was that he wasn't going to make love to her. He wasn't going to be the man who put an end to her innocence. He might be something of a jerk, but he wasn't that big a heel.

So you go back to the yacht and finish out the honeymoon, then tell her that she'll have to go along with things until filming is finished and you can get a damn divorce of convenience.

He walked back into the suite, leaving the sliding glass door open so the evening breeze cooled the spacious suite. Then he slowly approached the bedroom he shared with Kelly.

How had she gotten to him? he thought as he looked down on the bed. She was stretched out across the middle of it, her arms around one of his pillows, sleeping deeply. For a fleeting moment, he wondered when the wall of pillows had come down.

There had never been that much of a wall between them.

He'd let her get that close because he'd known, deep in his heart, from the very beginning, that she would never deliberately hurt him.

But fate was funny.

He listened to her gentle breathing, watched the soft rise and fall of her chest through the sheer white cotton nightgown.

He loved the fact that she had a sense of wonder about life, that she believed in miracles, that she still thought a happy ending was possible.

Where had that resilience come from? And why did he sometimes look at her and believe they might have a chance?

I don't believe in miracles, he thought wearily as he watched her sleep. *I can't.*

But somewhere deep inside, he knew he was starting to change.

Chapter Nine

"Derringer's Dame Devises Diva's Demise."

The imagined tabloid headline amused Kelly. She would have been the first person to admit she had an extremely quirky world view. She just hadn't often been in a position to slow down and enjoy it. Now, in the last week of her stay aboard *The Aphrodite,* she needed that warped sense of humor to see her through the moments with Donnatella.

The woman was driving her crazy. Donnatella knew she'd lost Steve, but she just didn't seem to have it in her heart to give up gracefully.

What did Dimi see in her, anyway? She was always flaunting her infamous, overblown body at the crew members, then glancing at Dimi to see if he was watching. Kelly thought that, as kind as Dimi was to her, Donnatella should have shown him some simple courtesy. At least.

Today, while sunbathing out by the pool, Kelly groaned inwardly as she spotted the diva, resplendent in a black bikini, making her way toward the pool area.

Not again....

To take some of the pressure off herself, she'd begun to visualize her relationship with Donnatella in screenplay format, mentally improvising whenever the woman was near.

Fade In:

Ext. Pool—Day

DONNATELLA approaches the pool, clad in a skimpy black bikini. The crew's eyes are bulging out of their heads. KELLY, cool as ever, glances up, her gaze hidden behind her sunglasses. She grimaces, then buries her head in the latest tabloid Dimi has so thoughtfully provided her with. DONNATELLA swaggers up next to her and stands at the foot of KELLY's chaise lounge.

DONNATELLA.
Mind if I sit down?

KELLY (*inwardly fuming*).
Be my guest.

She watched carefully as Donnatella dramatically lowered herself into a chaise lounge and took her tube of expensive French suntanning lotion out of her bag. She glanced over at Kelly, a look of disdain on her patrician features.

"You're still using that tropical garbage?" Donnatella remarked, her tone one a person would use with a particularly dim-witted child. She darted a look over at the table by Kelly's lounge chair. "I don't know how you can stand the smell. It's quite overpowering."

Ext. Pool.—Day

DONNATELLA goes flying into the pool, sun-tan lotion and all, as KELLY snaps and pushes her into the deep end....

I'm going off the deep end....

"I like the way it smells," she said, trying to keep her temper in check.

"I'm sure you do."

Kelly ignored her, deep in a tabloid story concerning a child star who had recently held up a 7-Eleven.

"Why do you believe that trash?" Donnatella asked, seemingly determined not to be ignored.

"If you'll recall, I never said I believed it. I simply read it."

"Why?"

"It's a gold mine of ideas."

"You mean you simply copy things?" Both amusement and contempt laced her voice. "How original. *That's* what your idea of writing is?"

"No, I don't simply copy things." Kelly wondered if she'd end up on the front pages of the tabloid again if she punched this woman out.

All Kelly wanted in the last few days she had with Steve was to relax. She didn't know what was going to happen once they both left Dimi's yacht, she only knew she'd fallen desperately in love with her husband.

But with Donnatella around, there was no such thing as peace and quiet.

"I still can't understand how Steve could have married a woman as provincial as you are."

"Believe it," Kelly muttered under her breath.

"What was that?"

"Donnatella." Kelly laid the tabloid down on the table between them. "I know it doesn't look like it, but I'm trying to get some work done and I'd appreciate some silence. Now, would that be too much to ask, or am I going to have to return to my suite?"

There.

Donnatella sulked in silence for all of three minutes.

"You'll have horrible tan lines if you leave your top tied that way."

Kelly glanced down at her bikini top, forgetting her resolution to completely ignore this woman. The bikini, a bright emerald confection that Luis had picked out for her, fastened around her neck and back with thin string ties. But the top was substantial enough that it would remain where it was even if she did loosen the fastenings around her neck.

She'd do anything to shut this woman up.

She unfastened the ties, tucked them out of the way of her prospective tan and returned her concentration to the article at hand. Several people who had known this child star for years were of the opinion that "I could see it coming a mile away. You know, she'd been headed for trouble for quite some time now."

Donnatella's voice shattered the silence.

"You wouldn't have any tan lines at all if you simply sunbathed the way we do in Europe."

Kelly glanced over. Donnatella, oiled and clad in nothing but the black bottom of her thong bikini, was stretched out on her lounge chair, like a deadly panther dozing in the sun.

"I'm fine, Donnatella. Don't worry about me."

"Oh, yes. I'd forgotten how provincial your tastes are."

That did it. Glancing covertly around to make sure none of the crew was around, Kelly untied the back of her top and swiftly rubbed some suntanning lotion over her front. Then she gave Donnatella a glare, wiped her sticky hands on her large beach towel, picked up her tabloid and settled down to read.

She was vaguely uneasy, several minutes later, when her instincts started working overtime. Donnatella had stopped nagging. She'd accomplished her objective, but what harm could there be in a little topless sunbathing in a private area in the middle of the Aegean?

STEVE COULDN'T STOP staring at the French tabloid.

Bernard, Dimitri's private steward, had thoughtfully dropped it off at their suite. Steve knew the man didn't have a malicious bone in his body, and malice had certainly not been his intent. He'd simply wanted both of them to peruse this particular article in private.

The *National Star*'s staff had obviously rushed the issue in order to have it on the stands by Monday.

The headline was bad enough.

"Derringer Dame Doffs Duds!"

But it was the series of pictures that was really getting to him.

Kelly's body was as beautiful as he'd imagined it. Clad in nothing more than the bottom of her bikini, stretched out sinuously on the lounge chair, she looked like any man's erotic dream brought to life.

And here he was, married to her and he couldn't touch her.

She'd be upset with the pictures when she saw them, but he'd assured her that the U.S. edition her friends and relatives would see would have black marks over the most incriminating parts of the photos.

Both of them.

It had been bad enough fantasizing about what he'd been missing, but to see it in a photo spread in living color was torture of a most peculiarly masculine form. Being a totally visual sexual animal, now he knew what he was missing.

Steve tossed the paper onto the coffee table in the corner of the suite. He knew his resolve not to touch Kelly was wearing thin. After all, she loved him and he cared for her more than he'd ever cared for any other woman. If they made this a marriage in more than name only, where was the harm?

He'd almost talked himself into it when his conscience intervened.

She wants it all. She still believes in miracles, like maybe you're going to be able to love her. And she doesn't deserve anything but the best. . . .

He heard the scratch of her key in the lock, and glanced toward the luxuriously appointed bathroom.

Another day, another cold shower.

As he locked the bathroom door behind him, he thought about what he was going to do with her.

If he brought her with him to the house he was going to rent in the Hollywood Hills for the duration of filming, he'd be on the set all day and she'd have the house to herself while she wrote. They'd have long periods of time away from each other. Maybe the feelings he had for her would settle down.

And maybe the sun would rise in the West tomorrow morning.

At any rate, once they were off the yacht, they wouldn't be living out of each other's pockets.

Thank God they only had a few days left of this enforced togetherness, he thought as he turned on the cold water full blast. He didn't know how much more of this honeymoon he could stand.

"DARLIN', I THOUGHT you looked *fabulous!*"

"Oh, you would!" Kelly replied, glad Aunt Bette was taking her public exposure so well.

"Cousin Patty almost had a coronary when she saw you on the cover! She subscribes, you know, so she got to break the news to the family back East. It made her feel so important!"

"I'm glad something did," Kelly said dryly.

"Darlin', don't be upset. No one that matters thinks any less of you. I myself think it's a hoot! I couldn't *believe* the ruckus! Why, Patty's so jealous, she thinks you're livin' the life she reads about in all those glitzy books of hers! I wish I was!"

"Thank God she didn't see the French edition."

"The *French* edition? *Ooh-la-la!* I think I'll give Patty a call this afternoon and *really* give her somethin' to worry about!"

"Bette!" But Kelly couldn't help laughing. Her aunt was incorrigible, and their prim, Southern branch of the family back East offered her an endless supply of amusement.

"Come on now, Kelly! They think you were raised by wolves to begin with, and they laughed when we moved out West 'cause they didn't have the courage to leave. They *wanted* you to fail, honey. Now they just can't stand it that you're gettin' a little piece of your dreams, and I can't stand not rubbin' their noses in it, just a little."

"I understand." Kelly paused, then rushed on. "I'll be coming home in three days."

"I'll?"

She swallowed against the sudden tightness in her throat. "I'm not sure we'll still be together. Technically, we've both finished our parts of the original bargain."

She could feel her aunt thinking furiously on the other end of the long-distance line.

"Well, the way I see it, you've got some choices to make. Now, don't let anyone tell you different. Women usually make the major decisions in relationships, and men are just relieved that they have some idea of what the hell's goin' on."

"You think so?"

"I *know* so. I think you need to ask yourself some questions, then make some major moves."

"Like?"

"Like, do you want this man?"

"Oh, Bette—"

"Now, don't get all ashamed or anythin'. That's just nonsense. What's between a man and a woman— when it's good—is about the only thing that makes life tolerable. And I *know* it makes things a lot more fun. Do you want this man?"

"Yes."

"Do you love him?"

"Yes, I think I do."

"Good. That always make things better. Now, do you think he loves you?"

"I don't know. I always catch him looking at me with the strangest expression—"

"Good, good. Strange expressions on a man's part means you're makin' some progress. Do you think he's confused?"

"Yes."

"Excellent. Now, what's goin' on the last few days you're on that yacht?"

"I think Dimi's going to throw some sort of farewell party."

"Oh, that man! He has *such* style! Now, you and Steve will obviously be goin' to this little event together, right?"

"Right."

"Well, then, get him to notice you. And, honey, with most men, you've got to be downright *obvious*. Now, remember that dress Rita Hayworth wore in *Gilda?* You need somethin' like that. Somethin' spectacular, like that glittery thing Luis poured you into. Maybe not gloves if it's a casual event, but you have to look drop-dead gorgeous."

"Hmmm."

"Make him yours, Kelly! Make the man sit up and take notice of you! You've been too nice, too compliant, too...too..."

"I get the idea."

"There's a bad girl in every woman, just waitin' to get out. And men love bad girls."

They discussed her wardrobe in detail, and finally picked out the dress. It was a wild, tropical print, with no back and very little front.

"Lots of makeup. And wild hair. Men love wild hair. Wear yours down, and muss it up like you just got out of bed. It'll give him *ideas*—"

"Oh my God..."

"Exactly. Put some condoms in your purse and watch out, world!"

Kelly was silent, thinking of what this sort of night could bring to fruition.

"Kelly? Are you still there?"

"Yeah."

"I know you don't have much experience. Darlin', you *do* want that to happen, don't you?"

"Yes. I just thought—"

"You thought he'd be in love with you first."

"Yeah."

"Well, let me give you two pieces of advice. The first one is, men use sex to get to love, and women use love to get to sex. And eventually, if you're lucky, you both sort of meet in the middle."

"And?"

"And my second piece of advice is that you'd have to be deaf, dumb and blind to let a man like Steve Delany walk out of your life! He needs you, Kelly, more than he needs those little pieces of fluff he's been datin'! I've been readin' the tabloids. I know who he's been goin' to those premieres with! Sex, sex, sex! Not that I'm knockin' it, but a man has to lay off desserts once in a while and tuck into a nice big plate of meat and potatoes, if you get my drift."

"What a flattering comparison."

"Now, darlin', don't be mad. He *needs* you. By seducin' this man, you'll be doin' him a *favor!*"

"Bette?"

"Yes, darlin'?"

"You could sell snow to Eskimos."

KELLY STILL WASN'T SURE what she was going to do by that evening. She was rereading more of her screenplay notes late that night, when Steve finally let himself into their suite.

"Hi." She studied him closely. "You look beat."

"Avoiding Donnatella is hard work."

"I thought she'd given up."

"So did I."

"That bad?" She set down the script. "I'm sorry."

"You and me both. Dimi has something up his sleeve for the last night of this little cruise, and I think Donna's going to make her move then. So stick close to me, okay?"

"Okay."

His gaze settled on the pieces of paper scattered all over the king-size bed.

"Working late?"

"I just can't seem to get a handle on my new hero."

"Tell me about him."

As she spoke, Steve shrugged off his shirt, then grabbed his pajama bottoms and sauntered into the bathroom. He continued to listen through the slightly open door, then came back in, ready to retire for the night.

"Do you want my honest opinion?"

"Absolutely."

"No man would ever behave like that."

"What do you mean? Like what?"

"You have him behaving like a woman's idea of what a man is like, and a man just wouldn't think that way."

"Then tell me how a man would think."

"He'd just . . . well, he'd just—*Damn*, Kelly, I can't tell you these kinds of things!"

"Why not?"

"You're so . . . innocent."

She arched one eyebrow at him. "Well, I've been doing a little thinking about that innocence, and I think it's costing me as a writer."

"What!"

"I mean, there's a whole side of life I know nothing about, a whole dimension of the human experience I haven't the foggiest—"

"Who is he?"

"Who is who?"

"This guy you're going to . . . experience this whole dimension with!"

"What guy?"

"Who is he?"

"Steve, now you're thinking like a man! I'm just saying it's something I've been thinking about, not that I've got some guy all lined up for the job."

"Oh. Okay. You just threw me for a minute there, Kel."

"I didn't mean to."

"I know. You're a painfully honest person."

Oh, if you only knew. . . .

"Okay, so how would this guy think about her?"

"First thought, first moment they meet? He'd want to nail her."

"Your language is so quaint. Is this really how men think?"

"You asked."

"When would he begin to see her as a person?"

"Soon after they started having sex. I mean, the whole physical thing is like a haze on a guy's brain, it's all he thinks about all the time. It's like an obsession. Once that first time is out of the way, he can get on to other things."

I'll be damned. Bette was right.

"So you think men and women don't think alike at all?"

"Let me put it this way. I've never met a woman whose train of thought I could even begin to fathom. And I guess that's kind of what makes things interesting."

"Even me?"

"Especially you."

"Thank you."

"For what?"

She chose to ignore his question, and countered with one of her own. "So he'd be much more aggressive in pursuing her, right?"

"Right. Unless—unless he had some sort of reason for not pursuing her."

"Like what?"

"Like she's off-limits for some reason."

"Like?"

"Oh, like his best friend's engaged to her, or she's like a little sister to him or she's—"

"A virgin?"

Tension hung in the air, thick as smoke. Hot as fire.

"That woman in your screenplay, she's not a virgin."

"No, she's not."

Silence.

"Don't do this, Kelly."

"Why not?"

He glowered at her. "Look, we've got just a few more days left, and I've kept my part of our bargain."

"Well, maybe I don't like our bargain anymore. Maybe I want something more."

"I thought you didn't have anyone picked out for the job."

"Maybe I've picked you. Eighty-seven percent of the women in America can't be wrong. And I'm fantasizing right along with them, but I don't even have a partner."

"Don't. Don't make up something in your head that can't come true. Don't imagine that it would be anything more than what it would be." The word he bit out made her wince, but she held his gaze with her own.

"How romantic."

"Sex isn't romantic," he said, his voice harsh. "Not when there isn't any love involved."

"Who said anything about love?"

"This isn't like you, Kelly."

"Maybe it's time it was."

"I'm not going to touch you. And don't you go off and find some Greek guy—"

"Maybe I will." She tilted her chin, hoping for a defiant angle. Her stomach was going crazy on her, and for a disastrous moment she thought she was going to lose her dinner.

"I won't let you."

"You're not my husband. Not really. Look, I'm not asking for everlasting love here, Steve. I'm simply asking for a roll in the hay. Think of it as an educational experience."

"Kelly!"

"Don't you want to?"

The look in his hazel eyes told her the truth long before he answered.

"It's all I ever think about. And you know it." He swallowed, and when he spoke again, his voice was low and harsh. "Don't go playing any games with me, Kelly. You'll lose, and you'll lose big."

"I don't think so."

"Don't bet on it."

And with that, he stalked into the bathroom. She heard him changing clothes once again, and when he came back into the suite he was clad in worn jeans and a pair of running shoes.

"Don't wait up for me," he said as he walked out the door.

"TONIGHT, WE PARTY!"

Dimitri held his wineglass aloft, and everyone else at the lunch table followed suit.

"And where are we going to do this, darling?" Donnatella purred. She'd been acting almost human with Dimitri the past few evenings, as if she had realized she'd pushed him too far.

"We're going to a taverna."

As Dimitri described the evening ahead, Kelly glanced at Steve. He seemed to be filled with a tightly coiled tension, there was a certain predatory stillness about him. Every so often she would catch him staring at her, as if she were a woman he'd never met before.

"Be ready to leave the yacht by six tonight, and be prepared to celebrate *all* night!" Dimi roared. He raised his wineglass to his lips, and everyone at the table followed suit.

SHE GOT OUT the dress, and barricaded herself inside the bathroom a good five hours before they were supposed to leave.

A leisurely bath. Shaved legs. Conditioned hair. A manicure and a pedicure. She suffered agonies of embarrassment before she picked out lacy black underwear, remembering Steve's reaction to the various clothes Luis had paraded in front of him.

She ordered a small carafe of wine sent to the room. She sipped some of it, then blew her hair dry and styled it. A full hour and twenty minutes before she was supposed to meet everyone else on deck, she started applying her makeup.

Steve hadn't returned to their room since that night. She supposed he'd found somewhere else to sleep, and she was grateful Donnatella hadn't found out about their estrangement.

Trust Steve to be discreet.

When she finally slipped the daring dress on, she didn't even recognize herself.

Backless. Almost frontless. The days in the sun had given her skin a burnished glow. Her eyes looked more alive, and she knew it was from loving Steve as intensely as she did.

Bette was right. Since she'd been a child, her aunt had advised her to dream big, then go after those dreams. And that was exactly what she was going to do tonight.

She heard the front door of the suite open, and drew in a deep, calming breath. So, even though Steve was mad at her, they were still going to present a united front.

"Steve?"

"In here. Almost ready?"

"I'll be right out."

She took another deep breath, adjusted the front of her halter dress over her braless breasts, glanced at herself in the mirror one last time, and sailed out into the main room of their suite.

Chapter Ten

"You're not going out in that."

"In what?"

"That dress."

"You don't like it?"

"Take it off!"

She started to obey him, a gleam in her eyes.

"No, leave it on! Go change. Right now."

"Kelly no do, master."

"Don't get smart with me. I'm not taking you out dressed like that."

"Oh, come on, Steve! Do you really think Luis would've helped me pack a dress that was unflattering or inappropriate? You're such a fuddy-duddy!"

"It's inappropriate because it's just a little too flattering."

"I married a fuddy-duddy."

"Kelly!" His tone was ominous.

"Well, look at it this way. Maybe I took your advice to heart."

"What advice?"

"Not to play games with you."

"You're playing games now."

"No, I'm not. I'm tired of living in this little glass cocoon of innocence. I want to break out and have myself some fun."

"No, you don't."

"Don't tell me what I want or don't want!"

"You don't know what you're asking for."

"Yes, I do. And maybe I can find a guy at the taverna who's man enough to give it to me."

Wrong, a tiny corner of her brain registered as an angry glint came into Steve's eyes. If he'd been mad when she'd snuck into his suite in Honolulu, that was nothing compared to this.

He started toward her, and she darted around the big bed.

"Get over here."

"Steve, not like this...."

"You want stud service, you got it."

"I didn't mean—"

"Fine. Then change, right now, or I'll do it for you. No wife of mine is going to be seen in a dress like that!"

"I'm not your wife!"

He turned, raking a hand through his dark hair in frustration. The expression on his face told her more clearly than words that he thought she was cracking up.

"I'm not your wife and I never will be. And all of my life I've put my emotional life on hold. Well, not tonight, Steve, for you or anyone else. I'm going out, *in* this dress, *to* this party, and you'd better be prepared to do me bodily harm if you intend to stop me!"

Anger that she knew had been simmering since the night he'd left their room now exploded.

"If it hadn't been for you and your big mouth, we wouldn't even be in this mess! 'Oh, Dimi, I just *lo-ove* the Greek Islands. I hope to get back someday.' If you hadn't mentioned that little tidbit, then we wouldn't be trapped on this yacht together, Luis wouldn't have picked out that damn dress and we wouldn't be in this mess!"

His imitation of her rankled. Her temper flared, and all Kelly could think of was to hurt him as much as he was hurting her.

"Oh, and you think your precious little Pammie would've done much better? I checked her out, I remembered her from a 'Love Boat' and a terrible monster movie! She couldn't act her way out of a paper bag."

Before he could even draw breath, she fired her next round.

"And where in God's name do you get off blaming this fiasco on me? 'Oh, Donnatella, *what* are we going to do? There aren't any movie theaters in this tiny little town.' After all, you're already doing it with eighty-seven percent of the women in America!"

"That's enough!"

"Well, I certainly hope so! If you'd had the brains of a billygoat in the first place and kept it in your pants, we wouldn't be in this mess!"

"That's it. We'll call Dimi and tell him we're not going—"

"Be as rude as you usually are. I'm outta here."

He grabbed her as she started toward the door.

She kicked him on the shin.

He released her and she darted toward freedom.

His hand closed over her wrist and he hauled her up against his chest.

"Don't do this, Kelly."

For a moment, she almost wavered. Doubt entered her heart.

But what's he offering you? a perverse little voice inside of her asked.

Nothing, she answered.

"Let go of me."

He slowly released his grip on her wrist, then let it drop between them.

"Damn it. Wear whatever you want. But try to be discreet."

His words stung, and she lashed out.

"Forget it. I'll change." Her hands went to the ties of her halter top, and she unfastened the secure knot. "One last question, Mr. Derringer."

Her use of his character's name caught his attention, and his hazel eyes narrowed as he looked down at her.

"Make it fast. Dimi's waiting."

"How come all you detectives are named after guns? Derringer, Remington, Baretta, Magnum. Is it some big macho phallic thing?"

"I believe that the writing staff comes up with our names. If there's any lack of imagination on that front, place the blame where it belongs."

She crossed her arms in front of her chest, holding up the front of the dress. Kelly could feel the furious beating of her heart. She'd never argued with anyone like this, and some instinct told her that in order for them to get to each other this violently, there had to be other feelings just below the surface.

I'm not giving up.

He was almost out the door. She'd decided to retie her halter top and wear the same dress when she called after him, "You know, you couldn't even pick a big gun, like a Magnum. A Derringer's a tiny little gun—"

The words had barely left her mouth when he was back beside her, his arms tight around her, pulling her blatantly against his body and lowering his head toward hers. The kiss was masterful, dominating; it left her weak in the knees and slightly dizzy.

It seemed to go on and on; he was moving his mouth over hers sensuously and not giving her a chance to think. All she could do was feel and react to the masculine invasion taking place. Her hands came up of their own volition and twined around his neck, partly in an effort to steady herself and partly in an attempt to get closer to him.

She could feel the softness of his cotton shirt, the roughness of his jeans. And she could clearly feel the strength and size of his arousal through the soft, silky material of her dress.

No Derringer there, she thought hazily.

He broke the kiss, and they stood next to each other, their bodies touching, their lips barely a fraction apart. Steve was breathing heavily, and she knew he was fighting for control the same way she was.

For an instant, she thought he might simply sweep her up into his arms and make that intimate decision for them both, and she wanted him to. But she watched as that rigid control settled over his features and felt his total emotional withdrawal.

"Derringers are deadly, little girl," Steve whispered at last, his fingers curled around her upper arms. He was practically holding her upright. "They're small because they're used for close work." His gaze focused on her mouth and she held her breath, waiting. "And used correctly, they're extremely dependable."

He let her go then, and her legs were shaking so badly, she almost fell to the floor. When he stepped away from her, she grabbed at the ties to the halter top with trembling fingers.

Steve was almost to the door when he glanced back at her. "Kelly?"

She looked up at him.

"And they fire twice."

THE FOOD WAS FANTASTIC, the dancers talented, the weather sublime, the music incredible—and Kelly was miserable.

She and Steve had sat in stony silence all the way to the island in the motorboat. Even Donnatella had noticed, coming out of her self-involved haze long enough to give Kelly a malicious smile.

Well, there weren't any movie theaters on this island, either, so they might as well have gotten to it.

Dimitri, sensing all was not right with the newlyweds, treated her with special care.

"You barely touched your food, Kelly. Was something not to your liking?"

"No. It was wonderful."

He hesitated. "A little fight?"

"A big fight."

"Marriages survive them."

"Not this marriage." She was too upset to care what she was saying. If Steve lost the part, then too bad for him.

"You think that. But each marriage has its ups and downs. You survive them, my dear. Don't make more of this than it is. Ask your husband to dance with you."

"I'd rather ask a pig to fly."

Dimitri let loose with a loud, roaring laugh, then afterward wiped his eyes. "I'm not making fun of you, Kelly, but you remind me of Tina. She had the same sort of temper. Once, early in our marriage, she went through a whole set of china."

"We would have understood each other perfectly."

One of the waiters hovered near their table, with a tray containing several small glasses.

"Try some of our ouzo, Kelly. After all, everyone should have a hobby." His dark eyes twinkled, and she suddenly felt ashamed, pouting and feeling sorry for herself when this man was trying so hard to ensure that everyone had a good time.

She glanced over at Steve. He'd deliberately sat at another table and was glowering at her.

Pooh. She took the small liqueur glass Dimi offered her, and swallowed its contents in one gulp.

FROM BAD TO WORSE. First, she'd insisted on wearing that dress. Now, she was deliberately getting drunk.

And around this crowd of lusty Greek men, that could be dangerous.

As worldly wise as she thought she was, Kelly was still naive. She had no idea how her friendliness and charm could be misconstrued. He thought about letting her find out the hard way, but even as the thought popped into his mind, he knew he couldn't do it.

He'd let her get all of this out of her system, keep an eagle eye on her, then calmly take her home.

After all, they were both adults. They could surely get through one more night in each other's company. Even if they hated each other's guts.

THREE GLASSES OF OUZO later, the world didn't look like such a bad place. In fact, she even thought about apologizing to Steve, the old fuddy-duddy.

But first, the bathroom.

Afterward, while looking at herself in the small cracked mirror above the sink and rummaging through her purse, Kelly came across the love potion she'd bought back in Honolulu. She'd slipped it into this same purse before they'd left, and it had fallen to the bottom, to snag inside the lining. She worked it loose, then held the tiny vial in her hands, wondering if she dared....

Why not? You've got nothing to lose.

She remembered the little Oriental man, and what he'd told her.

Very strong. Just a few drops, in coffee, tea or juice.

Coffee. That was it. She'd noticed one of the waiters pouring Steve an after-dinner coffee as she'd walked by his table on the way to the bathroom. She'd add an extra little kick, and maybe her mission would have a chance of being accomplished after all.

The night was still young. Hope riding high in her heart, Kelly swiftly powdered her nose, palmed the potion and snapped her purse shut.

Steve, you won't know what hit you.

HE SAW HER the minute she walked out of the bathroom.

Enough was enough. He'd apologize, but he'd make damn sure she understood that the position she put him in was absolutely impossible.

He couldn't be responsible for her losing her virginity. He grimaced. What he should have done was send her packing the minute he'd been informed of the fact. Virgins were nothing but trouble. He should have sent her after a unicorn, something simple like that. Anything other than this wild-goose chase.

Strange how the part didn't seem to matter as much anymore. Strange how the only thing he wanted, if he was truly honest with himself, was to make her happy. The thought that he wasn't up to it was the most depressing of all.

"Hi." She slid into the seat beside him, all tousled hair and twinkly eyes. The front of her dress barely covered one of her breasts, and he twitched the material into place, feeling oddly protective.

She looked as if she were about to pop, as if she knew some kind of amusing secret.

"I'm sorry, Kelly." The words were out of his mouth before he even thought.

"Me, too. About everything, especially calling you a fuddy-duddy. You're not, you know."

"No."

"You're a very sexy man. Let's kiss and make up."

She wound her arms around his neck and found his lips with hers. It was a short, brief, public kiss, but it did the job.

He couldn't see for just a second, it was as if a red haze descended over his vision. Then he gently pulled her away.

"This isn't the time or the place."

"How about the beach?" She winked at him—a perfect Nick Derringer wink—and he had to suppress the urge to laugh.

"You're drunk."

"I am not. It was just a little izzo."

His lips twitched. He had to stay in control of the situation, for Kelly's sake.

"Your coffee's cold. I'll signal the waiter." Before he could stop her, she put two fingers in her mouth and whistled sharply. One of the white-shirted gentlemen appeared at her side instantly, his dark eyes filled with humor. He'd sized up the situation immediately, and smiled warmly at Steve.

"More coffee?"

"Yes. We'll both have a cup," Kelly answered.

Once their coffee was poured and the waiter discreetly disappeared, Kelly leaned against Steve as she picked up her cup. He was calling himself all kinds of idiot names for refusing what she was blatantly offering him, when she whispered, "Look at that dancer!"

"Where?"

The man on the dance floor was executing an intricate set of kicks and spins. Dimitri was clapping in time to the music, and everyone was joining in, laughing and talking. Dimitri had grown up on this island, so whenever he visited his home, it became a celebration.

He felt her arm jostle his as she moved closer, then she was opening her purse and rearranging its contents. Her smile, when he glanced back at her, was brighter than ever.

"Drink your coffee, Nick."

"Steve."

"That's what I meant."

"It's still kind of hot. I'm going to let it cool off."

"Don't wait too long."

"Why?"

She seemed stumped for a moment, then said, "It'll get cold again."

He took her hand. "Let's talk about our marriage."

He was totally surprised when her eyes filled with tears. "Let's not."

"Honey, what's wrong?"

"You don't want me."

He leaned over and whispered into her ear, "I want you in the worst possible way. But we can't, and you know it."

"No, I don't. What's so awful about doing it with a virgin?"

"Lower your voice."

"Well?"

He hesitated, then plunged ahead. "Look, I know you think you can go through with this, and I think we'd both enjoy the physical part of it. But it makes things complicated, and the bottom line is that it'd be painful for you. Emotionally."

She looked down at the table, and he could just make out the tears filling her eyes.

"Kelly, don't do this to yourself."

"Am I that awful?"

"No, you're not. You're going to find some great guy who'll be everything you want in a man." Why did the thought make him so depressed?

"*You're* everything I want in a man. Just you. I don't care that you don't love me, I don't care that you can't give me what you think I need. All I want is you."

He put a finger to her lips. "Don't, Kel. You'll hate yourself in the morning."

"Not as much as I hate myself now. What did I do wrong?"

"Nothing. Nothing. Kelly, let's just get through this evening, and we'll get back to your room and then I'd like to talk with you—" He couldn't believe he'd even considered telling her the truth about his background, but now he knew it was the only way. "To tell you why it is that I don't think I'm the right man for you."

"Don't you dare patronize me." Her green eyes were slightly hazy, but he could clearly see the pride that burned brightly.

"I'm not."

"Good. Then I'm going dancing."

And with wavering steps, she started out toward the dance floor.

He was just about to go after her when a red-taloned hand grasped his elbow.

"Steve! Why, whatever has your little bride so upset?"

"Shut up, Donna."

Even Donnatella knew better than to cross him when he was in this kind of mood. He didn't take his eyes off Kelly. She'd approached a young Greek man, and he was smiling down at her. Taking her hand, he led her out onto the part of the floor that had been cleared for dancing. When he put his arm around her, Steve felt his jaw clench.

"My God, what a brute you become when you're around her. Are you always this primitive, Steve?"

"Only when I want something." He tore his gaze away from Kelly and focused on the older woman seated next to him. "What is it you want?"

"You know."

"The answer is no."

"Not even with Kelly out of the way? She doesn't seem very happy with you."

"Every marriage has its problems."

"But yours has so many, darling."

The mirth in her dark eyes slowly diminished as he stared at her, almost daring her to say anything else. In its place built a slow incredulity.

"You love her, don't you?"

That she could have seen inside him so clearly was astonishing. He'd thought Donnatella only cared about that part of the world that affected her, but he could see she was ready to finally give up on the idea of their ever getting back together.

"It was a weekend, Donna. Nothing more or less. I never lied to you."

"No, you didn't." Her smooth, tanned facial skin looked a little pale as she searched in her handbag for a cigarette. "Well, then, how about a cup of coffee together for old times' sake? It looks good."

"Take mine." He got up and left the table, then walked out the side door and down toward the beach. Whatever Kelly was up to, he didn't want to see it.

He wasn't abandoning her. Dimi wouldn't let any harm come to Kelly. He himself had already done enough damage.

EVEN ON THE BEACH, he couldn't get any peace. "Nick Danger?" said the short, squat man mending his fishing nets, as Steve passed him. "Bang-bang!"

He nodded his head and kept on walking.

And as he walked, he thought about Kelly. Many marriages started with a lot less, and they made it. Maybe she had enough love for both of them. Maybe, if he could get her back to Dimitri's yacht and tell her the truth, she'd understand what he'd been trying to tell her all along.

Maybe it wouldn't matter.

He'd walked about a half mile, and now he turned back, toward lights and sound and laughter. The music was faster now, the clapping louder and he could see the shadows of people dancing as he walked closer to the taverna.

"Mr. Danger?"

The short man had followed him, and now stuck out a ragged piece of paper and stubby, broken pencil.

A fisherman in Greece. Television stardom truly spanned the globe. Steve swiftly signed his autograph, then gestured toward the taverna.

"Why aren't you at the party?"

"Now I am. The net is finished."

Civilization had stood still on this small island. A fisherman's day wasn't over until he'd seen to his nets. Steve smiled, then clapped a hand on the shorter man's shoulder.

"Come on. We'll have a drink."

All thoughts of that drink were wiped out of his mind upon his return. The music, clapping and stomping had reached a fever pitch, and Kelly was in the center of it all, her skirts whirling as she twirled around on top of one of the small tables.

The scene registered with vivid clarity. The long length of her suntanned legs, the multicolored skirt flaring up, the briefest glimpse of French-cut, black lace underwear...

It was the underwear that drove him over the brink. That, and the fisherman.

"That is your woman?" he asked incredulously, following Steve's enraged glance. "How can you, Nick Danger, let your woman do that?"

How, indeed.

He didn't even remember when he started through the crowd, pushing several chairs and even a table out of his way. Crockery shattered, glasses tinkled; then he was almost upon her. She looked up, startled, and he realized she had no idea the spectacle she was making of herself or the potential danger she was in.

He was only interested in getting her home.

He grabbed her legs, then her hips, lifting her bodily off the table and slinging her over his shoulders. She gave a quick little squeak of fear, but he didn't even hesitate. Ignoring everyone and everything, he strode out of the taverna and down the beach toward the waiting motorboat.

"Steve! Steve, put me down!"

"Like hell I will."

Leo, another of Dimitri's well-trained crew, saw them safely back to the yacht. Steve practically pushed Kelly up the ladder and was over the side of the yacht and on the deck behind her before he heard her heels tapping as she walked briskly back to their room.

"Kelly!"

She didn't even turn around, and that made him madder than ever.

"Kelly!"

She began to run, and he gave chase.

She was fast, and by the time he'd caught up with her, she'd locked herself in the bathroom of their suite.

"Open the door!"

"No!"

"Open it!"

"Go away!"

Absolute masculine rage at her shutting him out gave Steve the rush of adrenaline he needed to kick down the door. He heard her surprised scream; then she was backing up, backing up, farther and farther away from him until her bare back touched cool tile and she shivered.

"Don't come any closer."

"That's not what you said before."

"You're drunk."

"No, *you* were drunk. I'm hoping you're sober now."

"I don't want this."

"I don't care."

They were locked in combat, not touching, their gazes intent on each other. He watched her carefully, watched the rapid rise and fall of her breasts, watched the way they swayed gently beneath the thin material. That dress was a walking seduction, and she'd known it. And he wanted to know why she'd pushed him when things had been just fine the way they were.

"Why did you wear that dress?" His voice was hoarse, and it echoed in the large bathroom. She'd turned on the light above the sink, and they were both bathed in the soft glow.

She stood her ground, looked straight back at him, her breathing becoming less erratic and growing slowly steadier.

"I wanted you to—want me."

"You got me."

They stared at each other for a long moment, and he knew the exact moment when she accepted him. When the slight wariness in her eyes faded and was replaced by excitement.

Somehow, she'd gotten him exactly where she wanted him.

Exactly where he wanted to be.

Almost, he amended silently, letting his gaze roam over her body, settling first on her breasts, then at the tops of her thighs. Almost.

"Do it," she whispered.

He stood looking at her for almost a minute, a mere three feet separating them. Yet he knew if he took those final steps, things would be irrevocably changed between them.

"Just do it."

He couldn't have stopped if he'd wanted to. Steve closed the space between them, pressing her back against the tile with his body. He grasped her wrists in his hands, brought them up over her head and lowered his mouth to hers.

Chapter Eleven

It was the kiss she'd waited for her entire life.

The tile was cold against her bare back, his body was pressed warmly against her front. And every bit of feeling that he'd tried to repress went into that first kiss, firing her to life and making her reach for him, cling to him, submit to him.

She never wanted to let him go.

The kiss went on and on; he rarely took his lips from her mouth, her cheekbone, her neck, her collarbone, the tops of her breasts. Then the flimsy halter top was pushed aside and he was cupping her breasts, then kissing them, then taking the nipples into his mouth and arousing her to a fever pitch.

He untied her halter.

Her fingers trembling, she clumsily unbuttoned his shirt.

He reached beneath her skirt and tore off her black lace panties, then cupped her, his touch firm. Sure.

Her legs shook so badly, she almost slid down the wall.

He kissed her again, his mouth hot and firm against hers, his restless hands framing her face and holding her still, his tongue sliding inside her mouth and making her shake. His fingers were sliding through her hair. She grasped his shoulders with her hands so she wouldn't fall down.

It worked, her mind thought hazily. *That potion worked.*

Then his fingers touched her inner thigh, then higher, then he claimed her intimately and all rational thought flew out of her head.

She couldn't think, couldn't speak, couldn't do anything but break the deep kiss and rest her head on his chest. Her legs were trembling, she didn't think she could stand up much longer and she wanted...she wanted...

When he spread the soft folds and touched her, so gently, with the tip of a finger, she cried out, then buried her face against his chest.

It felt like a flame, his touching her so intimately.

It scared her.

He seemed to sense her mood, for he stopped and slowly moved away from her.

"Take it off," he whispered. His eyes never left her, she felt his gaze on her face, her breasts, her belly and lower.

She slipped the dress off, her hands shaking, and the vividly colored material pooled in a heap at her feet.

"The sandals."

She leaned down and unfastened them, then stepped out of them.

He was shrugging out of his unbuttoned shirt, but she glanced away when he reached for the fastening of his pants. She wanted it to happen, she wanted to ex-

perience everything with this man, but she wasn't sure
she would ever be truly ready for what was about to
happen.

Such a mystery. She knew the basic mechanics of
the act, but she didn't know how it would be with
Steve, what would arouse him, what he would do to
her, how it would feel. She'd had no idea what it entailed, making love with a man she loved so intensely,
and the feelings were overwhelming her.

She wanted to please him. She glanced up at him
and saw he was simply standing in front of her.

Waiting.

She recognized the look in his hazel eyes for exactly
what it was. Hunger. He wanted her.

They were going to make love.

They were going to have sex.

She couldn't romanticize it. He'd been honest with
her. But for just one instant, with both of them bathed
in the warm light of the bathroom, Kelly wished desperately that he loved her. It would have made it easier for her, just knowing.

But he hadn't lied to her, and she wasn't going to lie
to herself.

She held out her hand.

He took it.

He pulled her against him, and she could feel the
length and strength of his erection. She'd wondered
what his hair-roughened body would feel like against
hers, and she found she liked the sensation. His skin
felt warm, almost hot, as it slid against her. Leg to leg,
belly to belly, breast to chest, they were as close as they
could possibly be.

She'd thought he'd carry her to the bed, and was surprised when he simply lowered her to the plush rug next to the tub. They lay side by side, facing each other, and he held her against him as he touched her.

"Do you like this?" he whispered as he touched her breasts. She could barely breathe, the sensation was so exciting. She even liked watching his tanned hands against her breasts, her nipples taut and full, smooth as satin.

"Yes..."

She liked everything he did, all the ways he touched her, every intimacy he initiated. When his hand touched her again, he held her wrists above her head and prevented her from moving away from his touch. Sensation built, frightening, shattering, and she gave herself over to him and climaxed in his arms.

He held her as she felt herself floating back to him, and when she looked up at him, she smiled.

"Mmmm." Her face felt flushed, and she watched as he traced the blush over her shoulders and breasts with a finger.

"Did you like it?"

"Mmmm." He was lying on his side and she slid closer to him, then draped one of her legs over his thighs.

"Tell me what to do," she whispered. He'd given her incredible pleasure, and she wanted to do the same for him. She didn't want her ignorance to ruin things for him.

"Everything."

"But I don't know—"

"Shhh. I'll teach you."

He caught her hand and kissed it, then slid it slowly over his chest, over the rough hair. She didn't take her gaze away from his as he guided her hand lower, lower, until he closed her fingers over his arousal.

Her eyes widened. She hadn't known what she'd expected, but his body was so hot, so hard. He kept his hand over hers as he taught her to pleasure him.

When he took his hand away, she continued to caress him.

"Hmmm." He leaned back, his eyes closed, tight lines of tension around his mouth. She wanted to kiss them away, but she concentrated on touching him, almost afraid to improvise.

When he stopped her, his reaction was so swift, she started.

"What did I—"

"Nothing. Nothing." He shifted his body so he was over her, sliding between her thighs. "You're perfect." He kissed the tip of her nose, then her cheek, then teased her mouth, coaxing it open and enticing her to respond.

It was so easy. It was so frightening. But she loved him so much, and she wanted to give to him.

He smiled down at her, his weight on his elbows, and studied her face long enough for her to become self-conscious and feel her cheeks turn pink.

She glanced away. "Don't."

"Don't what? Look at you?" He kissed her neck, then whispered, "I like looking at you. You're so beautiful."

"No—"

"Yes." He kissed her neck, her mouth, her temple.

"Can we turn off the light?"

"No."

She bit her lip as apprehension flooded through her. He buried his face in her hair.

"Don't you know what you to do me?" he whispered against her ear, his lips tickling her. "Can't you feel how hard you get me? Kelly, you can't do anything wrong when it's all so right."

He feels it, too. He knows it's more than...it's more than... Her heart leapt in her throat and she reached up and touched his hair, stroking its softness gently. Emotion overwhelmed her, and she knew without a single doubt she'd made the right decision.

She'd wanted to wait for an extraordinary man, and she'd found him.

"I want you so much." Her words came out on the gentlest sigh, and she sighed again and moaned softly when he pressed his hips against her, answering her silently, telling her how much he needed her.

"I've wanted you for a long time," he whispered, raising his head. "C'mere."

"What?"

"Kiss me."

She did, rolling with him so they were side by side again, the thick rug comfortable against her bare skin. His hands moved over her breasts, her belly, then lower until she was mindless and whimpering.

When he slid down between her thighs and kissed her, she almost climaxed again.

"Steve!"

He grabbed her wrists and held them. "Don't. Let me."

She couldn't stop him, couldn't stop the sensations from flooding her body, couldn't stop her response. It happened again; she felt as if she were straining against the limits of her body. She closed her eyes, deep inside herself, and then she shattered, holding his hands tightly, not wanting him to ever let her go.

This time he didn't wait for her to come back, but slid up her body and moved inside her. She felt his penetration, smooth and hot, felt him completely inside her, filling her.

He moved, gently, slowly. So carefully.

He made love to her, and she opened her heart and her body to him, wanting him, loving him, knowing this moment would stay with her the rest of her life.

She felt so attuned to him, to each shift in rhythm and pressure, to the subtle changes in his breathing. Then she couldn't focus on him at all as he seemed to touch her deeper and deeper, brighter and hotter, finally taking her over the edge yet another time.

Afterward, panting, she looked up at him and found him smiling down at her, the warmest expression in his eyes.

"Steve, I—" *I love you.*

He must have seen it in her eyes, because he kissed her, stopping the words as he thrust harder and harder. Her hands low on his body, her fingers clutching his buttocks, she held him against her as he reached his release. The power and beauty of it stunned her.

Later, curled against his chest, both of them tucked into their large bed, Kelly stared into the darkness and knew that Steve had been right.

Physically, it had been wonderful.

Emotionally, everything had changed. And she wasn't sure she was strong enough to endure those changes.

Everything was different. A deep loneliness threatened to engulf her. It seemed so strange that they'd been so close, and now she felt so very distant from him.

He wasn't asleep. She felt the slight pressure of his hand against her waist. Her cheek against his chest, she wished she had the courage to tell him how much she loved him, how much she wanted to remain with him. Kelly had no idea what was going to happen when they left the yacht, and the thought of never seeing Steve again was devastating.

"Kelly?" His voice was low and so very soft.

"Yeah?"

"You okay?"

The truth trembled on the tip of her tongue, and she longed to tell him how she really felt. Then she thought of how gauche and unsophisticated she would appear, how much trouble she'd already caused him.

Though she wanted to speak from her heart, she couldn't.

"Sure."

They lay in silence for almost a full minute, then Kelly spoke up.

"Was it . . . okay?"

In silent answer, he took her hand and moved it low on his body, to his full arousal. Excitement trembled through her as she realized this small amount of power she had over him.

It would have to be enough. For now. It wasn't time to speak from her heart, but to make more memories.

She shifted beneath the cool sheets, moved against him, then laced her fingers in his hair and pulled his mouth down to hers.

When he broke the kiss, she could hear the smile in his voice as he whispered, "No more Derringers?"

"No." He was about to kiss her again, and she couldn't resist the urge to whisper, "But you do fire twi—"

He silenced her with a kiss.

SHE WOKE UP the next morning, sore in muscles she hadn't even known she possessed. Glancing over at the man responsible, she found him sleeping peacefully. She'd woken several times during the night to simply watch him, and it had been almost dawn when she'd realized that Steve Delany was no longer a restless sleeper.

Now, knowing he was about to wake up, she realized she had absolutely no idea what she was going to say to him.

What did one say to a man who had completely turned your life around? How did you thank someone for opening you up emotionally and making it possible for you to take the ultimate intimate plunge?

How could she be casual and talk to him as if they were still buddies, when she loved him with all her heart?

She decided to take it in baby steps, and choose the easiest way out. Sliding out of their bed, Kelly crept to the bathroom. She thought about closing the door behind her, but it had broken off its hinges.

She needed time to think.

Once alone, and on the site of what was her most emotionally wrenching experience, all her doubts came back in full force. He wouldn't want all her emotions, he wouldn't want to hear what she felt, how she felt about him, how she didn't want to leave him, couldn't leave him, couldn't imagine a life without him— *Stop.*

She stepped into the shower and turned it on. The water was warm and comforting, and Kelly reached for a bar of expensive French soap. She was lathering her shoulders when she realized she was crying.

What am I going to do?

Dropping the soap, she leaned back against the cool marble shower stall and began to sob.

HE WOKE UP with a sense of well-being he hadn't even known it was possible to possess. Steve stretched, then reached over for Kelly. He would have made love to her in a second, but he didn't want to wear her out her very first time.

She was gone.

He heard the shower running, and he smiled. She was probably shy about seeing him after last night. He'd have to reassure her that everything was all right. What he felt for her was the closest to love he would ever feel, and he had a strange hunch that she'd understand.

He'd tell her the truth. Everything. Today.

It was a liberating thought. He'd carried it all with him, inside of him, for so long. It was time to let it go. He'd realized, late at night, lying next to her in bed, that he was never going to let her out of his life.

He needed her, and that terrified him.

He wanted her. That was patently obvious.

He...loved her. And he'd fight heaven and earth before he'd lose her.

Steve stood up and stretched, then padded over to the bathroom and silently eased past the broken door. He had almost opened the frosted glass shower door when he heard the choked sobbing.

Everything inside him went very still as he tried to imagine what she was feeling. He thought of what he'd taken from her as shame suffused him.

It didn't matter that she'd thrown herself at him. It didn't matter that she'd driven him crazy, tempted him, practically demanded that he make love to her. He'd been older, more experienced.

There was absolutely no excuse for what he'd done.

Quietly, each small sob tearing out a piece of his heart, Steve backed out of the bathroom.

"AH, TO LOVE A WOMAN enough to break down a door for her. Those were the days." Dimitri smiled at Kelly from across the breakfast table, and she valiantly summoned up a smile in return.

"I'm sorry about the door."

"Nonsense! I'm just happy the two of you decided to settle your argument. You see, I was right."

She was going to get through this breakfast without breaking down, even if it killed her. Concentrating on buttering a flaky croissant, Kelly deliberately changed the subject.

"Where's Donnatella? I didn't see her on deck this morning."

"I left her at the taverna."

"What!" For just a second, Kelly even forgot about Steve. "What happened?"

"She went crazy over one of the waiters, and was not her usual devious self. I cannot abide a woman making fun of me, so I let her go."

Kelly pondered this for a second. Dimitri looked so composed, as if he broke up ten-year-old relationships every day. But he had to be hurting. As badly as Donnatella had treated him, they had been fond of each other.

"Are you—how are you feeling?"

"Better than I have in years!" Dimitri's dark eyes sparkled with life as he faced her. "I should have finished it with Donnatella a long time ago, but she had become a habit. And a costly one."

"Will you be all right?" It surprised Kelly to find out how much Dimitri Alexandros had come to mean to her in the few weeks she'd been on his yacht.

"I'll survive. And it gives life a more interesting edge, to be searching for the right woman all over again." He sighed. "Though I'll admit, I envy Steve. His search is over, and he found the perfect woman."

She could feel tears welling up in her eyes, and fought to hold them back.

"You know, don't you, Kelly, that if Steve hadn't already chosen you for his bride that I would have made my intentions very clear."

"I know."

"But now I consider you a friend. A member of my little family, as it were. And I don't feel that way about many people."

She smiled at him then, overwhelmed at the friendship he was offering her. "Thank you, Dimi. I'd like to feel the same way about you."

"Then if you need anything . . ."

How much did those dark eyes really see? she wondered.

Though Kelly was desperate to talk to someone about what had happened between her and Steve, she couldn't betray her husband's trust in her.

"I know." She forced her gaze to remain calm and steady on the older man's face. "And if you need anything, you only have to ask."

"Just a good woman."

She smiled. "I'll see what I can do."

"Good. Now, we eat."

But she barely picked over her fruit salad and café au lait, her thoughts on the husband she'd left back in their honeymoon suite.

AFTER BREAKFAST, Kelly walked over to one of the far railings overlooking the sea, her purse clutched firmly in her hands.

It's not nice to fool Mother Nature.

Why had she ever thought of putting that stupid love potion in Steve's coffee? How had she ever thought either of them would benefit from her manipulations?

She gazed out over the Aegean, the bright blue water glittering in the sunlight. It blurred in front of her eyes.

Through both her stubbornness and her selfishness, she'd had a wedding night after all. Steve had been honest with her, and unwilling to involve himself emotionally from the start. But she'd pushed and pushed and pushed—

I'm so sorry....

She gazed at the water for a few more minutes, lost in thought, then concentrated on searching through her purse until she found the vial. She gave the tiny bottle one last look, wishing she'd never thought of asking the little Oriental man to prepare the love potion for her. Then, before she could change her mind, she flung it into the sea with all her strength.

She watched the vial flash in the bright morning sunlight before it hit the water and was swallowed by the dancing waves. Hopefully the potion would sink straight to the bottom where it wouldn't do anymore harm.

"Kelly."

Steve. The moment she'd been dreading. Well, she couldn't avoid him for the rest of the trip. They still had a little more time on the yacht together. The least she could do was behave in a cool and collected manner and not break down like a baby.

Taking a deep breath, she turned toward him.

He looked as nervous as she felt. For a split second, she thought she saw beyond the usual personality Steve allowed her to see, to the man he really was beneath.

He looked tired. A little nervous. Even scared.

"Kelly, I'm sorry...."

Hearing him say the actual words was so many times more horrible than she'd imagined. Though making love with Steve had torn her apart emotionally, Kelly knew she'd never be sorry for the choice she'd made.

Never.

"It's okay," she said softly. "I understand."

"No, you don't. I just—I wanted you to know..." He was suddenly, awkwardly, inarticulate. It touched her. Steve Delany, alias the glib Nick Derringer, at a loss for words. It made him seem more human somehow.

It was a pity there weren't screenwriters for moments like these. These conversations always looked so effortless in the movies. In real life, the pain was overwhelming.

"It's okay. It wasn't your fault."

"No, it's not okay. You trusted me, and I betrayed that trust."

"No, you don't understand. I made you drink that love potion."

She could tell, from the look in his eyes, that she'd lost him again.

"Love potion?"

"The one I got in Honolulu."

"What?"

"It was meant—I thought I'd—I wanted you to love me, and—"

"Wait a minute. Where was this love potion, and what are you talking about?"

She told him the truth, ending with the fact that she'd distracted him long enough to slip a few drops of the herbal concoction into his coffee last night.

"So what you did—I don't hold you responsible for what you did because I...I guess I drugged you or something."

He was laughing.

She couldn't believe it; he was laughing.

She started to walk away from him, darted past him one way, then the other. He blocked her escape, then took hold of her arm and gently but firmly kept her close, right next to him.

"I didn't drink that coffee—but I think Donnatella did."

"What!"

"I was angry, and I left. She wanted to have a cup of coffee with me for old times' sake, but I told her to simply take mine."

"Oh my God."

There was a short silence, filled with meaning, as both of them thought about the possible consequences of taking the love potion.

"He left her at the taverna," Kelly said.

"Dimi did?"

"Because of a waiter."

"I'll be damned. I guess you did Dimi a favor, after all."

"It worked." She was stunned, thinking that a few drops of a potion had managed to break up such a rich and powerful couple.

If only I hadn't thrown it overboard....

But even as much as she'd disliked the woman, Kelly hoped nothing too bad had happened to her. Her thoughts were interrupted as she glanced up at Steve. The way he was looking at her, the intensity of the emotions behind his gaze, totally took her breath away.

"But I don't understand. About last night..."

"I wanted you. There's no potion in the world that could have made me want you as much as I already did."

"Oh."

She wanted to tell him he hadn't betrayed her, that he'd given her the most wonderful night of her entire life, but fear kept her silent. She swallowed, trying to work up the courage to tell him, but his next words silenced her.

"I just wanted you to know it will never happen again."

Something inside her died then as she looked up at him, standing in front of her in the bright sunlight. How strange, that she should love this man so very much, and that everything, including his own emotions, should conspire to keep them apart.

She touched his arm reassuringly, determined not to let him see her heart was breaking.

"I understand."

She wouldn't bother him anymore. Their time together was over, the deal was done and the least she could do for both of them was to leave the relationship without making an utter fool of herself.

"Kelly, I wanted to talk to you about—"

"No." She held up her hands as if to ward him off while smiling brightly. "It's okay. It really is." The thought of Steve trying to come up with some sort of emotional consolation prize for her was too much to bear. She couldn't take crumbs when she'd wanted it all.

"I wanted last night, and I'll never regret what happened between us." She hated the way her voice was starting to wobble, but she continued past the tight pain in her chest and throat. "But I think we've both honored our original agreement."

When Steve didn't answer, she whispered, "Time's up, Steve. It's a done deal. We don't need each other anymore."

He was staring at her, his dark hazel eyes disturbingly intent.

"Is that what you think?"

"That's what I think."

Silence stretched between them, and she wondered how she could have felt so close to him last night and so very far away from him now.

He touched her cheek with his hand, and she fought the impulse to lean into him and rest her head on his chest. She blinked, willing away the moisture welling up in her eyes.

"You're sure?"

She'd leave this relationship with some shred of pride if it killed her. Like Ingrid Bergman in *Casablanca*.

"Yes."

He kissed her then, on her forehead, his hands on either side of her face. She closed her eyes, savoring this last small physical contact. Then she watched him walk across the deck, away from her and out of her life.

THEY'D BE LEAVING *The Aphrodite* in a matter of hours.

Steve walked the deck alone that afternoon, watching the sunlight play over the sparkling sea.

Done deal, my foot. It ain't over 'til the fat lady sings.

He'd think of a way to keep her with him. It was as simple as that. Dimitri was such an eccentric, it wouldn't be that hard to come up with something.

He's Greek—they don't believe in divorce.

That'd work—if Dimi hadn't already been divorced. Twice.

If you leave this marriage now, Dimi will know it was a fraud. He'll be furious and find someone else for the part.

Just stay with me until filming is over. . . .

Filming would take at least four months. In that time, he'd be able to come up with some excuse to keep her with him.

The only thing he was absolutely sure of was that he didn't want to let her go. He smiled as he looked out over the brilliant water.

Oh, no, Kelly. The deal's not done. Not yet.

Chapter Twelve

Crumbs didn't seem so bad, when you led with your heart.

Kelly thought about this almost a month later, securely ensconced in Steve's rented house high in the Hollywood Hills. She'd decided to spend the day rearranging the kitchen cabinets—anything to get away from writing her current screenplay.

It wasn't going smoothly, but when had her characters ever deferred to her wishes? It was a rare project that was visited by the muse, and even though Kelly firmly believed in parking her butt in her office chair for a certain amount of time every day, there were certain working days she recognized for being what they were—totally worthless.

Thus, she'd decided to distract herself with housework.

"Darlin', I'd settle for not even having your life if I could just get my hands on this kitchen!"

Bette was helping her paper the kitchen cabinets. Kelly had always gone all out wherever she'd lived, even if she didn't own the property. You could live in a rental for months, even years, so why not have it exactly as you liked it?

Dimitri had helped them find this house. Actually, he owned it and was renting it to Steve for a song. Well, for free. Kelly had just decided to give up and consign the millionaire to the rank of guardian angel.

It was a spectacular kitchen, as befitted a spectacular house.

"Just like that wonderful old house in *Dead Again*," Bette had said when Kelly had walked her through it. "I wonder if you and Steve knew each other in a past life or somethin'."

Please. We have enough trouble in this one.

The house had been built in the forties, during old Hollywood's heyday. Perched on a hillside, it was all dark wooden floors and pale stucco walls. Kelly loved it, and felt at home in it instantly. It was a house to dream in, a house to love and cherish and fill with laughter.

The kitchen was one of her favorite rooms, and she spent a great deal of time here during the day. At night, she always left Steve a generous portion of the dinner she'd cooked in the fridge, ready to microwave. But when she heard the sound of his rented red Porsche in the spacious driveway, she quit whatever she was doing and headed for her separate bedroom, where she carefully spent the remainder of the night.

Doris Day would have understood the situation perfectly. There definitely wasn't any *Pillow Talk* going on in this house.

Not that she hadn't thought about it.

The old aphorism was true—there were some things you didn't know you were missing, and for a virgin, incredible sex was one of them. But now she knew, and she also knew she'd been lucky enough to escape the bumbling, fumbling legions of ordinary men and be initiated by a master.

"You're thinkin' about him, aren't you?"

Kelly snapped back to the present and stared at her aunt.

"Weren't you?"

"Yes."

Kelly knew her aunt was waiting for her to confide in her, but she also knew Bette was sensitive enough not to push. And this whole situation was something Kelly didn't want to talk to anyone about. Not yet.

Not when she couldn't figure it out herself.

He'd caught her a few times, usually days when she'd been out sunning by the pool and he'd come home early. There were days like that, when he wasn't needed in the next few shots. Kelly had her master endurance plan ready to go; she'd been serene and calm and gracious—

And escaped to the sanctuary of her bedroom as soon as possible.

Cried in her private shower.

Pounded the goose-down pillows on the bed.

Decided to hate him forever.

And rejected that notion immediately. She loved him.

She *missed* him. She missed him so much that the feelings overwhelmed her. All the time. Every waking moment. Every minute, lying in her bed and unable to sleep.

She channeled all her energy and frustration into her work. Steve was still shopping her original screenplay around with the help of a friend, an excellent agent at one of the most prestigious agencies in town. And Kelly, never one to rest between projects, had almost finished her second screenplay.

She'd had to fight the urge the story was taking, to parallel what was going on in her real life, even though the bargain she and Steve had made was an incredibly complicated plot. This second screenplay was coming along quickly; she'd have it finished in a matter of weeks.

All of her life she'd wanted to be in a situation where she could give her work the best she had to give and not worry about the bills. Now here she was, sitting in the lap of luxury, and even though her work was progressing smoothly and she was closer than ever to achieving her dream, there was a part of her that was unhappy.

Well, at least someone's going to benefit from all this. Dimitri will have the most organized kitchen in the Hollywood Hills.

She and her aunt worked in silence, listening to Oprah and her guests on the thirteen-inch color television on the counter.

"—But when he ran off with my little sister after emptying out my checking account and totaling my car—"

"Twit!" Bette sniffed. "Where do they get these people? If I'd been her, I would have punched him in the nose and booted him out the door."

Kelly looked at her aunt with new eyes, after having been married almost two months.

"Bette, how come you never got married?"

"Shoot, sugar. I did. You and Colleen just never heard about it 'cause the family kept it hushed up."

"*What!* Who?"

"Jimmy Delgado."

"Jimmy Delgado!"

"It was his eyes." Bette smiled, a dreamy expression on her face. "He could just look at a girl and you'd know what he was thinkin'. And if she had a brain in her head, she'd be thinkin' the same thing. He was Italian or somethin'." Bette made this last statement as if it accounted for everything.

"What happened?"

"Well, we ran away, got married, got to the White Pine Motel and had a few days of fun before your Uncle Carl and my Daddy found us."

"And—"

"And they were right. Jimmy had another wife a few towns over. My heart was broken, but at least I got a wedding night." At this, Bette gave Kelly a pointed look.

She refused to rise to the bait.

"Did you love him?"

"I thought I did. That was enough."

"Why'd you run away with him?"

Bette sighed. "It seemed like a good idea at the time. It turned out just like *The Captain's Paradise* with Alec Guinness. But not as funny."

They worked silently, papering the cupboards with the pale blue-and-white paper Kelly had picked up a few days ago.

"How's Steve's movie goin'?"

"Good."

"I cannot believe Dimitri cut Donnatella off like that! Even firin' her off the picture! But I suppose Steve's relieved he's workin' with a less temperamental actress. Was that article in *Us* magazine the truth?"

"Most of it."

"Well?"

"Steve likes working with her." Donnatella's loss had been Genie Bouchet's gain. The dark-haired, New York actress was well on her way to getting her first big-screen break. Steve had confided in Kelly that what he'd seen of her in the dailies had been incredible.

I'll bet he is, too.

Bette left soon after the kitchen was completely finished. Kelly sat in the large room, watching the sun leave it and the shadows softly start to grow. It saddened her to think that she and Steve lived such separate lives in this house. It shouldn't have been that way.

The thought of eating dinner alone tonight was abhorrent to her, and she walked over to the dining room table and grabbed her purse, then fished through it for her car keys. Steve had rented her a car, and even though she'd insisted on something relatively sensi-

ble, he'd seen through her and picked out a silver
Mazda Miata.

Dimitri had also thought to leave a British green
Jaguar XKE at her disposal.

It was almost funny, seeing both cars parked in the
spacious driveway. She loved both men, in different
ways, but would have taken the bus if there'd even
been a chance of Steve falling in love with her.

Kelly went back into the kitchen and sat on one of
the bar stools by the counter, wondering who to call.

Not Bette. Too much time with her too-perceptive
aunt and she'd be sobbing all over her shoulder.

Colleen had recovered from her surgery completely
with the amazing resiliency of the young, and was
deeply immersed in a whole new group of friends.
Kelly had watched as she was relegated to a sideline
position, but she'd been so happy. Everything was as
it should be for her little sister.

Luis. He'd come out to the coast to do Steve's
makeup on a photo shoot. There was a chance he was
still here. She dialed the number of his condo in West
Hollywood and he picked up on the third ring.

Within minutes, she was out the door.

THEY DECIDED on a tiny Italian restaurant just off
Sunset. Kelly managed to fool Luis into believing she
was eating her half of their Caesar salad, but when she
barely picked at her ravioli pesto, he knew something
was up.

"I like a girl with a healthy appetite, and you usually have one. What's wrong?"

She knew she could trust him. She knew he'd never tell a soul.

The story took them through their main meal and into cappuccino and tiramisu. Luis listened carefully, letting her talk, while deftly maneuvering her untouched dinner into a doggie bag for lunch tomorrow.

She sat looking at her cappuccino afterward, totally depressed.

"He's a complex man, your husband."

"He's not my husband."

"He is. More than he even thinks he is."

They sat in silence for a few minutes, then Luis said quietly, "I knew the two of you were going to be good for each other, but I didn't know how hard it would be along the way. I'm sorry."

"It wasn't your fault."

"Not my fault, sending you to a nightclub with him at your ravishing best? Making you look gorgeous on your wedding day? I consider myself culpable. By the way, darling, your skin is terrible. You've got to try and get a little sleep."

"I know," Kelly whispered. She'd never felt this heartsick in her entire life. "I wanted to stay with him, and now all I do is ignore him. I wanted him to love me, but I almost think he dislikes me—"

"No. No." Luis took another sip of coffee, and seemed to be weighing his words. "He's lost everyone he loved, Kelly. He's frightened of losing you, so he's pushing you away."

"I don't think so."

"You don't? Whose idea was it for you to stay on? Steve doesn't need to be married anymore. Word on the street says he's brilliant in the film, and both Dimi and the director are ecstatic."

She stared at Luis across the table, and hope began to fill her, hope that she might have a chance after all.

Just one more miracle. Please.

"He just sort of—moved me in."

"Close, but not too close."

"Yeah."

"Listen to me. He gave Colleen a chance. He's giving your screenplay a chance. Kelly, give him this film. Let him show the world what he's truly capable of, let him reach for his big dream. But don't ignore him, Kelly. He's a Leo, and Leos live for love. You'll break his heart."

"You think he's... he's just as scared as I am?"

"I know he is."

"But what if we... what if we end up..."

"In bed? *Quelle horreur!*" Luis wiggled his eyebrows.

Their waiter came by, unobtrusively, and Kelly noticed that the restaurant's crowd was thinning out. They'd been sitting at their table for almost three hours.

"We'd better get going."

"Kelly." Luis caught her hand again. "I'm not the sort of man who gives advice to people, because I don't usually take it myself. But I do know one thing. Love and friendship are the most important things on this earth. What we are to each other. How we care.

He reaches millions of people and makes them happy, but you're the only one who can reach him.''

''I don't understand.''

''Just love him. That's all you have to do. You're going to have to open your heart and love him completely, love him before he loves you. That's just the way it has to be with Steve.''

She must have looked doubtful, because Luis leaned across the small table and took her other hand in his.

''Just love him, Kelly. It's all any of us really want, and what everyone needs.''

STEVE WAS IN the kitchen, rummaging through the refrigerator when she got home.

''Hi,'' she called as she breezed in. He looked up from the refrigerator, and he seemed slightly wary.

''Hi. How was Luis?''

So he'd seen her note. ''Fine. We went to that little Italian place he likes.''

''Did you have a good time?''

Was that the tiniest bit of jealousy she detected?

''Yes. I did. Did you eat?''

Simple questions. Caring questions. Questions a husband and wife might have been asking each other for eight years instead of almost eight weeks.

''Not yet.''

''I've got a ton of ravioli in this bag. With basil and Romano cheese.''

He smiled, a tired, lopsided smile, and her heart turned over. He was too tired to be Nick Derringer; he was simply Steve.

''That sounds good.''

He opened a bottle of wine while she heated the pasta and found a loaf of good French bread. There was lettuce in the greenhouse, and by the time Steve was seated at the table, pasta in front of him, she had made a salad.

"This is very good."

"It sounded good."

"You didn't eat?"

"I wasn't hungry."

"Eat some of it now."

Warning bells should have sounded. It was too intimate, eating off the same plate, sharing a salad, watching him cut her another piece of bread. But she decided to throw caution to the wind, and poured herself a second glass of wine.

Afterward, she made a pot of coffee and found the last of the brownies she'd made the day before. Without stopping to think about what she was doing, she carried a tray with dessert and coffee into the informal living room.

There was a plush couch there, as well, facing the enormous fireplace. Many cool evenings, when Kelly knew Steve was going to be working late, she'd lazed on this couch in front of the fire, a good book her only company.

Now, she watched as Steve lit a fire, then sat next to her on the sofa while she poured coffee for them both.

"Brownie?"

"Thanks."

He ate two of them, then sipped his coffee, all without looking at her. She wondered at what Luis had told her, and wondered if he was as nervous as she was.

She thought of asking about the film, or about Genie or Dimi or Luis, but nothing seemed casual enough. She set her coffee down, and decided she was going to risk her heart, just a little.

"I've missed you."

His gaze locked with hers, and she saw everything she wanted to see in his face. Except love.

She bargained with her heart, her emotions. If Luis was right, she'd have to be the one to give, at first.

"I miss you, too," he said, his voice low. "And I don't blame you for hiding from me."

They'd both set down their coffee, and sat facing each other on the sofa. Tension permeated the air again, came up between them so effortlessly. Kelly wondered if it would always be this way between them, or if it was simply because what both of them wanted was so impossible. Forbidden.

Whatever it was, what both of them were thinking wasn't very wise.

"I thought you might be pregnant—"

"I'm not—"

"I've always been responsible before—"

"I didn't give you much of a chance—"

They both stopped, remembering that long night, their last night aboard Dimi's yacht.

"Let's talk about you, Kelly. Let's decide that you'd better leave this room. Because I may not be capable of loving you, but I sure liked sleeping with you."

He almost got her with that one. For a wild moment, she thought of packing her bags and never, ever coming back.

But she couldn't.

And she realized at that exact moment that love didn't give you a choice. She knew, looking at Steve, that she would get to the bottom of this, and if he didn't want her after that, there would be no one else for her.

"I liked it, too." She swallowed again. "That's part of what I miss."

"Then we agree on something. Why don't you come to my room tonight?"

The implication of what that made her was almost too much, but she rallied.

I'm not going to let him push me away, she thought, forcing her chin up, her shoulders back.

"I'd like that," she whispered, deciding to take him by surprise.

She did.

"So would I," he said, after a few seconds had passed.

"Don't you ever get tired?" she asked.

"What?" He was genuinely perplexed.

"Don't you get tired of running and hiding and keeping it all inside?"

"Don't try to psychoanalyze me, Kelly. You'll lose."

At that moment, fear left her, and she realized love was the strongest force of all.

Luis was right. She had to open her heart and love him completely.

"I can't lose if I care for you."

He glanced away from her, and she could sense the tension in his body.

She stood up, then looked down at him. Stepping away from the couch, Kelly gathered up their coffee mugs and dessert dishes. She walked to the kitchen on shaky legs and set the dishes down. At the kitchen door, she turned.

"If you want me," she said in a surprisingly even voice, "you can come to my bedroom. The door won't be locked."

She was halfway up the great curved staircase when he caught up with her.

He swept her up in his arms and carried her to his bedroom.

It was dark inside, and he didn't turn on the lights. He yanked off her clothing, shrugged out of his, then came down over her on the large bed.

It was different from the first time, when he'd wooed and cajoled and seduced her. This was fierce and totally masculine, as if he were trying to dominate her, master her, overpower what had happened between them by the fire. As if his lovemaking could wipe out all her thoughts, all her emotion, and leave just the physical relationship between them.

She wasn't afraid. She knew enough about what happened between a man and a woman, and she knew this man. He could try and pretend what she'd said hadn't affected him, but it would have been impossible. A lie.

The truth was almost as powerful as love.

She accepted him, and if he refused to let his heart enter into their physical relationship, she opened her own to every bit of feeling and emotion. She kissed him, her heart full of what she felt for him, and she felt the rage and fear leaving his body as he began to touch her, hold her in a different way.

She found the language of the body to be the most eloquent and she heard what he was trying to tell her without words. She knew when he crossed that silent line and started walking that emotional tightrope with her. She knew what it cost him as if they were two sides of the same coin, two parts of a whole. And she loved him even more for trying, when the stakes were so very high.

He climaxed above her, his body taut and straining, his head thrown back, all masculine power and fire. She accepted that part of him inside her and clutched him to her.

And as she found her own pleasure in the strength and heat of his body, Kelly knew that what had happened between them was far from over.

Chapter Thirteen

The only place they communicated was in bed.

Before Kelly knew it, she was sharing his room. They'd never spoken of their decision. It just happened.

The night after their confrontation, she'd retired to her own room. He'd found her there and brought her back to his. And they'd slept together ever since.

Strange, how two perfectly intelligent people couldn't seem to find words to talk about what was really important.

Kelly thought about what Aunt Bette had told her so many months ago. "Men use sex to get to love." Was that the case? Kelly couldn't be sure. She couldn't be sure about anything anymore.

At odd moments, Steve's words still haunted her. *I may not be capable of loving you, but I sure liked sleeping with you.* She sensed he thought of her as his greatest weakness, and their lovemaking was his way of trying to get her completely out of his system.

But the sexual side of their relationship was becoming more intense, not less. Steve's plan was backfiring, and it seemed to be making him angry with himself.

But how could loving someone ever be considered a weakness?

"Darlin', I just love your dress!"

She returned to the present with a start. Still clad only in her silk slip, Kelly glanced at the clock in the bedroom. The limousine Dimitri had sent for them would be coming within half an hour.

Time to turn into Cinderella.

The cast party Dimitri was throwing tonight after almost four months of filming was going to be the event of the Hollywood season.

"Entertainment Tonight" gave it quite a bit of coverage, as did all the news stations and gossip magazines. *Variety* and *The Hollywood Reporter* had both mentioned the event in their columns, and everyone who was anyone in Tinseltown wanted to be there.

Kelly didn't really want to go.

But she had to. It was the culmination of all Steve had worked for, and she wanted the attention to be on him and his incredible performance, not on the mess they'd made of this marriage of convenience. She had to do this for him, but afterward, she had a sinking feeling they wouldn't be together much longer.

Their marriage of convenience wasn't so convenient anymore.

He'd taken care of his part of the bargain. Colleen had recovered completely, and was a normal child in every sense of the word. One of the studios had taken out an option on her first screenplay, and Steve had promised to take her second script to the same agent.

And he'd finished Dimitri's film. The word on the street was that it was going to make him a star.

Kelly studied herself in the mirror, astounded that Luis could make her look so good when she felt her heart was breaking and her life was falling apart. The last thing she wanted to do was go out tonight, but she couldn't disappoint Dimitri. And Aunt Bette was over the moon at the thought of attending a real Hollywood party.

"Do I look all right?" her aunt asked.

Bette looked stunning. Her beaded dress and headband that Luis suggested were similar to what a flapper had worn in the twenties. On Bette, it looked divine.

Luis had come over and done their makeup and hair, too, and Bette had been almost overcome with excitement at having her face done by an actual Hollywood makeup artist.

For Kelly, Luis had decided on a rather Grace Kelly look. The evening dress was simple, a classic style like the one the actress had worn to the 1954 Academy Awards. He'd swept all of Kelly's wild, curly hair up on top of her head, miraculously tamed it into an elegant chignon, and adorned it with a single white rose.

It worked. His taste was flawless. As much as she'd wanted to wear something more daring or sophisticated, this look was just as sexy, in a different way.

Steve was meeting them at the cast party. One of the large studios had been completely transformed into a tropical paradise. There was to be a huge sit-down dinner, live entertainment and dancing.

A night to remember forever.

A night to finally realize that some dreams weren't meant to come true.

A night to finish their bargain.

Kelly knew it was only a matter of time before Steve asked her to leave and filed for divorce.

What could she say to make him give their marriage a real chance?

She glanced at the clock once again. Time was running out.

HE SAW HER the minute she entered the room.

For a while this evening, he'd thought she wouldn't show. But she had, and the action so suited Kelly. She was a fighter, and she'd see their deal through to the bitter end.

How clever of Luis, to dress her in white. He was sure his friend had done it as a symbol, a reminder of Kelly's innocence, and all he'd taken from her.

Tonight he was hoping she'd simply give up and leave him alone.

But she wouldn't. He knew it, and it caused a strange sense of despair deep in his gut. He watched her, her head held high, her eyes quickly scanning the huge, totally transformed studio until they lighted on him. She smiled, and when he didn't return her greeting she looked away and started into the room.

Life was funny. Until she'd barged her way into his hotel suite, he'd thought he'd known what bravery was. She might be playing havoc with his emotions, but she was still the bravest person he'd ever met.

She was immediately surrounded by the crush of people, and Steve tore his gaze away from her and glanced at the bartender.

"Another Scotch."

She nodded, deftly filling a glass with ice and pouring the liquor into it. He walked away from the bar, nursing both his drink and the sense of impotent rage that filled him.

Impossible. It couldn't be done. What she wanted from him wasn't in him to give. It had all been burned out, a long time ago.

Taking another sip of his Scotch, Steve watched Kelly as she made her way through the crowd. He knew what this whole relationship was doing to her. Exactly what it was doing to him.

So do I take the chance of losing her, or do I leave her before the inevitable happens?

He swallowed another mouthful of liquor, his body tense, his emotions tightly under control.

The deal would be finished tonight.

STEVE LOOKED WONDERFUL. Dark and dangerous in his suit, with that natural, incredible presence. Kelly had mingled, listening to scraps of conversations, smiling at everyone. But never for a moment losing sight of his presence.

The room buzzed with excited conversation. The word was, Dimitri's movie was going to make Steve Delany a star.

We both got what we wanted out of the deal...then why am I so unhappy?

Because she hadn't counted on falling in love.

She didn't have to study the crowd to see the women vying for Steve's attention. He was playing another part tonight—his public persona. Kelly was sure that this part, and Nick Derringer, were the roles that women swooned over.

The funny thing was, she'd fallen in love with the real Steve Delany. The man who wore reading glasses in bed. Who sang—quite badly—in the shower. The guy who liked eating Ben & Jerry's Chunky Monkey ice cream out of the carton in front of the refrigerator.

The man who'd taken her virginity, captured her heart, and was probably going to leave her before the evening was over.

She thought of the picture she'd found, almost a week ago. Snooping was not in her nature, but when she'd found the faded black-and-white photograph in his drawer, she'd picked it up.

Two little boys. She recognized Steve as the elder of the two, and the younger boy holding on to his hand had to have been Billy.

Something about those smudge-faced children had torn at her emotions, and she'd carefully put the photograph back in the drawer, exactly the way it had been. She'd never mentioned it to Steve—not that they ever talked, anyway.

But she couldn't help wondering about that picture, and what had transpired in Steve's life to make him the man he was today.

"Hold still, darling. You're losing your rose."

Luis came up behind her, and with a few swift ministrations, he fixed the back of her hair.

"You look wonderful in that suit."

"You can't go wrong with Armani. Come with me while I freshen my drink."

THE INTERMINABLE EVENING was almost over.

As was their marriage.

Dinner had been finished for almost an hour, and Dimi had given several toasts. To the production staff, to the actors, to the writers, to the director. Kelly had noticed that Bette was sitting next to him, and she caught her aunt's eye and smiled encouragingly.

She'd introduced Bette to Dimitri earlier. The two of them had taken one look at each other and sparks had been ignited; Kelly had watched two of her favorite people in the world find each other.

She and Steve had sat together at Dimi's table, but as soon as it was politely possible, Steve had gotten back up and started circulating again.

The musicians were tuning their instruments, and Kelly decided that a quick trip to her favorite refuge, the ladies' room, was the idea of the moment. She planned on taking a few deep breaths, fiddling with her makeup and trying to figure out what she was going to do next.

Shelley Adams, Steve's publicist, waylaid her before she got to the restroom.

"What the hell is going on with you and Steve?" she hissed under her breath. "The photographers haven't been able to get one good photo of the two of you together. Either you're on opposite sides of the room or you look as if the two of you are at a funeral! Now find him and look happy, or I can't guarantee what the tabloids will print."

"Leave her alone, Shelley."

Steve. He'd come up behind them, and neither had noticed him.

"Come on, Steve, you need to push this picture," Shelley continued, this time urging him.

"It's okay." Kelly was surprised by how steady her voice sounded. "Where do you think they'd like us to pose?" She attempted a smile for the publicist. "I'm not really used to all this. I don't think I'm very good in crowds."

"Honey, just look at Steve with those adoring little eyes, and they'll eat it up. Follow me."

She didn't dare look at Steve, but he stayed by her side, his arm firmly around her as they negotiated the crowd. Once in front of the photographers, they answered some questions and posed for pictures. Most of the attention was focused on her husband, and she simply pretended she was the other half of a happily married couple.

It was absolute torture. The man she loved embraced her, kissed her, smiled at her—all for the benefit of the camera.

They were almost finished when a young male photographer called, "Hey, Kelly! Look this way!"

She flashed him her best smile, determined not to ruin this night. It was the last part of her bargain with Steve.

Flashbulbs popped, filling the corner of the studio with brilliant light. The press had liked her from the start. A shot of Nick Derringer's bride always boosted a magazine or newspaper's circulation.

"Still in love with your husband?" the photographer called good-naturedly.

She looked up at Steve, and thought she saw a flash of emotion in his eyes before he became the Daring Derringer the public so loved.

"Very much," she said softly.

THE PARTY BROKE UP soon afterward.

"I'll take her home," Luis offered. Kelly was reaching for her wrap, and it seemed to her that he was giving Steve a challenge.

"No, she goes home with me. She is, after all, still my wife."

Steve's words had been spoken softly, for Luis's benefit alone. He and Bette were the only two people who knew the truth about their marriage bargain and who wouldn't be surprised when it ended in divorce.

Bette had come up to her earlier in the evening, and confided that she was going with Dimitri to one of his favorite clubs. Kelly marveled at the unlikely pairing of her aunt and Dimitri, but was delighted with the start of their new relationship.

Now, driving home late at night in Steve's Porsche, Kelly wondered when he was going to tell her theirs had come to an end.

She didn't have long to wait. Once inside the house, he took her hand and halted her flight to their bedroom.

"Kelly."

She couldn't look up at him, now that the moment was at hand.

"I think it's time we ended the deal."

Chapter Fourteen

"I know."

He hadn't expected that answer.

"I don't want to leave, but if you want me to, I'll respect your wishes."

"I think it would be best."

"I don't—but I'll go. On one condition."

She could feel his tension, a palpable sensation in the silent house.

"What?" His voice was flat, as if all the emotion had drained out of his body.

"Why? Tell me why."

That made him go completely still, and Kelly knew they'd reached the critical crossroad. Now it would be played out to the end, and she didn't know how it would turn out. But she knew she would fight, she would seek out the truth and—whatever it was—she would love him for the rest of her life.

"Fair enough." He walked over to the liquor cabinet and poured himself another glass of Scotch.

"You know about my brother Billy."

"Yes. But Steve, I saw the picture in your dresser—"

"What!"

"By accident. You and Billy. And I know it must have been horrible, your mother dying when you were so young...."

"What the hell are you talking about?"

"That picture. Billy's clothes were too small. Your shirt was held together with safety pins. It's no sin to be poor, Steve. It doesn't mean—"

"My mother...my mother is still alive."

She stared at him, knowing instinctively that the missing piece of the puzzle was almost within her grasp.

"She gave birth to both of us before she was nineteen. Her family wasn't much help, and neither were the guys she chose. I never met my father, and I don't even know if Billy and I had the same father."

Kelly couldn't believe what she was hearing. She'd grown so used to thinking of him living in that sunny house in Oregon with his parents and three siblings that she couldn't picture his early life any other way. Without asking, she knew he'd never had those other brothers and sisters.

Only Billy

"So one day she decides to take Billy and me out for a while. She took us to a movie, then the circus that same evening." Kelly couldn't breathe. She knew this story couldn't possibly have a happy ending. "I thought it was the beginning of us trying to make ourselves into a family. I thought..."

He paused for such a long time she had to bite her lip to keep from speaking.

"At the end of the day, when we got home, the family services people were there, waiting. They'd decided she wasn't capable of taking care of us, so they... took us to a home."

Tears filled Kelly's eyes as she tried to imagine two grimy little boys, their confusion and terror.

"She told me to take care of Billy."

The family in Oregon disappeared forever.

"How old were you?" she asked quietly.

"I was four. Billy was one."

The silence was so loud she could hear her heart beating, sickeningly fast.

"We were there for almost five years. I spent most of my time defending Billy. Kids can be cruel, and I beat the snot out of anyone who looked at either of us the wrong way."

She could barely breathe, the pain in her chest was so intense. She'd wanted the truth, and now wondered if she could bear to hear it.

"This home got by with minimum care, but I kept thinking that if we could just hang on until Billy was a little older, we could escape."

She thought of him, so young, so helpless, spinning desperate dreams. She thought of herself, so young, trying to take care of her sister.

"I got punished for beating up one of those bullies," he continued. "I mean, pick on me, don't pick on Billy. They locked me up in this cupboard. One of those kids got hold of Billy. They forced him to stay outside all night. It was cold and he caught pneumonia. They didn't bother with a doctor and he died."

Tears filled Kelly's eyes and she wiped at them with her evening wrap. She felt Steve kneel beside her and cup her cheek in his hand.

"You told me that story about your sister and I thought, if there is a God, maybe I was being given a second chance. Maybe I could make it up to Billy if I helped Colleen. But I swear to you, Kelly, I never meant for the rest of it to happen."

"I know." Her throat felt so tight, she could barely force the words out. His eyes were so sad, and she knew for the first and perhaps last time she was seeing past the carefully constructed facade to the real man inside.

"You want a miracle, Kelly, and I can't give it to you. I can't risk losing someone I love, again."

She'd waited to hear those words for so long, imagined what it would feel like hearing them from Steve. Kelly wasn't even sure if he was aware of the implications of what he'd just said, but she did know one thing.

He was sending her away.

"I'll know you're out there, and I'll do everything I can to make sure your script gets sold. But I think it's time the deal was done."

SHE SPENT THE REST of the evening packing.

In a little less than five months, her entire world had been rocked off its foundation. She didn't know what Steve planned to do about their marriage, but she knew she'd never be the same.

After their final conversation, she went straight up to his bedroom and pulled out one of the suitcases he'd bought for her to take aboard *The Aphrodite*. She would have used her old one, but Steve had thrown it away. Kelly pulled the drawers out of her side of the dresser and dumped the contents inside the case.

He'd told her to take everything he'd bought her, but she only packed a small suitcase with absolute necessities. She had to leave, had to get away from this man she loved with all her heart but who couldn't love her and didn't want her there.

She reached the bottom drawer, and pulled out the envelope containing her second completed screenplay.

It's his.

She held the heavy manila envelope in her hands for a moment, thinking of how many hopes and dreams were wrapped up within the printed pages. Thinking of how she'd hoped her marriage to Steve wouldn't end in divorce.

Maybe that was why she'd decided to be a writer. When it was just you and a keyboard, you could guarantee a happy ending. And happy endings were important, when life threw so many things in your path.

She put all her notes into the large envelope, then sealed it and wrote Steve's name on it. She'd leave it for him; she had no doubts he'd make sure it reached the proper hands.

By the time she was finished, the bedroom looked as if she'd never inhabited it. Sitting down at her desk, she pulled out a piece of stationery and a pen. She'd write Steve a note and leave it with the screenplay.

Kelly stared at that blank piece of pale blue paper and tried to figure out how to find the words to express what was in her heart. It wasn't even necessary to tell him that she loved him. Somehow, she was sure Steve already knew.

She wrote the words quickly, before she had a chance to change her mind. A single sentence. And afterward, staring at the written words, she realized there was nothing more to say. She folded the paper, slipped it into an envelope, sealed it, then picked up both the letter and the larger envelope and stepped out into the silent hall.

Where was he?

She found him asleep in the room she'd once occupied. He looked exhausted, dark circles beneath his eyes, his skin so pale. His breathing was deep and even, as he slept the sleep of the truly exhausted.

Kelly stood at the foot of the bed and looked at him for a long time, knowing it would be the last time she'd ever see him. After tonight's revelations, he couldn't possibly want to see her again.

She'd asked for the truth and he'd given it to her.

She wished she could have had his love.

Back in the master bedroom, she thought about calling a taxi, but the events of the night were catching up with her. Exhausted, she set the alarm for six in the morning, struggled out of her evening gown, then curled up beneath the blankets and closed her eyes.

STEVE WOKE UP an hour later, at almost four in the morning. He was about to go take a shower when he noticed the large manila envelope on the nightstand by the bed.

Kelly.

He opened it and scanned its contents. A screenplay. He riffled through it, wondering what she'd decided to write about this time.

He held his feelings at bay, carefully keeping them pushed down. Funny, the one thing he hadn't counted on was how much it had hurt when she left. But he still had a small part of her in the pages in his hands. Picking up his reading glasses and slipping them on, Steve started to read.

Two hours later, he set the screenplay down on the nightstand and let out his breath in a long sigh.

When he gave that screenplay to his agent, Jeff Robson, it would change Kelly's life forever. This script was going to set Hollywood on its ear.

Her first script had been good. Excellent, for a beginner. But there had been that sense, reading between the lines, that the author was still a little young and naive.

Innocent.

Something had happened to her during their time together. All the laughter and confusion, the pain and pleasure, the tension and fighting and incredible sexuality, everything she'd experienced while they'd struggled to achieve their dreams had exploded out on to those printed pages. It was an absolutely compelling script, filled with emotion.

And he knew it would make her a star.

He certainly wouldn't take credit for creating her, a Henry Higgins to her Liza Doolittle. But they'd both packed a lot of living into the past few months, and it couldn't help but affect her view of the world.

The guilt he'd carried since the night he'd taken her virginity suddenly lifted. He hadn't been able to give her a relationship, but he'd given her something of value she'd take away with her, something she could use for the rest of her career. He'd given her an intense taste of life, and Kelly had grabbed that brass ring for everything it was worth.

Steve swung his legs over the side of the bed, thinking about a hot shower and a cup of black coffee, when he noticed the pale blue envelope on the carpeted floor.

He picked it up and opened it.

One sentence. One sentence that summed up the most incredible time of his life.

I wish it could have been different, but I'll never regret the time I spent with you.

The enormity of his loss hit him then, flooded his body. He closed his eyes. The huge old house in the hills seemed so empty. He'd loved coming home to her, even on the nights when she'd hidden in her bedroom. Just knowing she was there had been enough.

The way she fought with life and tilted against her personal windmills. Her belief in the absolute goodness of life. Her faith in miracles. The way she wrinkled her nose when she smiled, the sound of her laughter, the mischievous glint in her green eyes.

The feel of her skin, her scent, the warmth, the absolute giving over when they'd shared a bed.

Kelly was unlike any woman he'd ever met.

He knew, at that exact moment, that there would never be anyone for the rest of his life who would occupy the place Kelly had so effortlessly taken. There would always be a part of his heart that would belong to her, but as Steve closed his eyes and fought with his emotions, he tried to convince himself that he'd done the right thing.

But none of it seemed to make sense anymore.

He thought of something Genie Bouchet had said. He'd gotten to know the actress on the set of Dimi's film. Her husband Pierce had brought their three children to the set several times, and Steve had marveled at the way their family worked so well. It was something so foreign to him, he appreciated it when he saw it.

One day on the set, while waiting for the lights to be set up, he'd asked her what it was like, being a mother. Her answer had been simple. "It's like having a piece of your heart walk around outside your body."

Loving Kelly felt the same way.

His eyes were wet when he opened them and stared down at the letter in his hands.

And he realized that Kelly wasn't the only one who had been profoundly changed.

THE ALARM WENT OFF promptly at six and Kelly called for a taxi.

She couldn't face going home to her empty studio apartment, so she decided she'd stay with Bette and Colleen for a few days. She needed to be around people who loved her, needed to be in a safe place where she could break down in private. Then she had to figure out what she was going to do with the rest of her life.

She washed her face, dressed, brushed her teeth and hair, then picked up her suitcase and purse and headed out the door. One last time.

STEVE WAS JUST DUCKING beneath the stinging shower spray when he heard the front doorbell ring. He turned the water off. Had Kelly come back? And then he heard her voice.

"I'll be right down."

She's still here!

He reached for a towel and swiftly knotted it around his waist, then ran to the bedroom window. This particular bedroom overlooked the front of the house, so he glanced down to the flagstone drive.

A bright yellow taxicab was parked in front. Its young driver, dark-haired and with the build of a weight lifter, was slinging a small suitcase into the trunk. Kelly stood beside the car, looking down at the pavement in front of her. Even her bright, wavy hair seemed subdued.

Last night she'd surprised him, crying when he'd told her his story. For a moment, he'd thought of trying one more time, but then fear had engulfed him and he'd rejected her.

Now, seeing her standing in the driveway, he knew that once she got inside that taxi, he'd never see her again.

But you love her.

Wasn't that enough?

His bare feet started moving before he made a conscious decision, and before he knew it he was racing down the stairs, slamming out the front door and coming face-to-face with a very startled Kelly.

"Who the hell are you?" Steve said, facing off with the taxi driver.

"Hey, you're that Nick Danger guy!" The taxi driver was incredulous, then delighted.

"Derringer!" Kelly and Steve said simultaneously, both annoyed at the intrusion.

Now that the crucial moment was at hand, Steve couldn't seem to get his brain to work.

Kelly glanced up and simply stared.

Steve Delany. In a towel. Muscles glistening with water. Dark hair wet and slicked off his face. Hazel eyes studying her intently.

She took all this in within the space of a heartbeat. But one impression registered above all others.

He was unnerved.

No, she thought. *Upset* would be a better word.

He took a step toward her.

Perhaps *devastated,* Kelly thought as she turned and opened the taxicab door.

"Stop!"

Her feet kept moving.

"Stop, damn it!"

Move feet, move.

He tackled her, and they both slid to a heap on the flagstone drive.

"Man, this is just like that episode with the dog-nappers! Remember that one, Nick?"

Then the knot came loose, the towel fell off. And she was on a driveway with Steve Delany, and he was as naked as the day he was born.

She closed her eyes, deeply embarrassed.

He picked up his towel.

"Kelly, I—" He couldn't stop looking at her face, and the thought of never seeing her again was like a sharp knife twisting inside his gut. She gazed steadily at him with those green eyes, but even though she'd been startled by his sudden appearance, he didn't see hope flare in them.

He'd taken care of that.

"I don't want a miracle, Steve." Her voice sounded rusty, almost flat, as if she hadn't used it for a long time. "I just thought maybe we could take it day by day, a little at a time—"

He took hold of her hand, then pulled her into his arms. He held her as if he couldn't bear to let her go.

"I know I pushed you and tried to force you to love me, but I didn't mean to hurt you."

"Shhh." He stroked her bright, coppery hair and wondered how he could have ever envisioned a life without her. She'd had so much faith in him, she'd believed in him when everything logical had told her otherwise.

He had a feeling Kelly was going to get her miracle after all.

"There won't ever be anyone else for me."

"I know," he whispered, his voice low and rough. "I know. Me, too." He glanced over at the taxicab driver, who was leaning against the hood of his cab. He was staring at them and wiping the tears from his cheeks, his dark eyes filled with emotion.

"Could you get her bag out of the trunk?" Steve called out, pulling Kelly tighter into his arms.

"You got it, Nick." Within seconds, Kelly's suitcase was next to them on the flagstone driveway, and the taxi driver was backing away, his hands up in the air in apology.

"I won't charge you guys. I mean, she really thought she was leaving and all—"

"No, wait a minute. You spent time driving up here." Steve reached for his pocket—and felt the towel. He laughed, and Kelly said, "I got it." Keeping tightly to his side she rummaged in her purse and came out with a twenty, and handed it to the driver.

"Thanks!" He was almost to his cab before he turned around. "Hey, Nick, I know it's a bad time, but could I get your autograph for my wife? Jeez, she loved that show."

Steve looked down at Kelly, and she'd never seemed more beautiful to him. Her hair was tousled around her face, her green eyes were flooded with happy tears, her cheeks and nose a shiny pink.

"Up to you."

She nodded her head.

He adjusted the bath towel, knotted it securely, then got up and walked around the cab to the driver's side. And for the first time in his life didn't feel he had to hide behind the Derringer persona.

"How about on this piece of paper here?" The taxi driver was rummaging through the mass of fast-food wrappers and magazines in the front seat of his cab.

"I've got a picture," Kelly called out. While both men watched, she unsnapped her suitcase and pulled out an eight-by-ten glossy.

"Oh, this is gonna be *great!* Sign it, 'To Danielle, from Nick.' Wait a minute, could you put 'To *Tony* and Danielle, from Nick'?"

"Sure."

"'Best wishes'?"

"You got it."

As Steve signed the picture, Tony lowered his voice and said, "Happens all the time, and usually right about now."

"Huh?"

"You been married what, six months?"

"Almost five." Steve still looked confused.

"They all run home to their mothers. It never lasts, though. You gotta be firm, know what I mean? Let them know who's really the boss."

"They are," Steve said dryly.

"You're right about that, pal." Tony collected his autographed picture, thanked both of them profusely, then jumped into his cab and gunned the motor.

"You got out here in the nick of time!" he called, delighted at his joke.

"Thanks, Tony!" Kelly called after him. Steve glanced over at her and saw a smile back on her face, and he knew he'd spend the rest of his life keeping it there.

"You need a cab, you ask for me. Tony Danilo. I'll give you guys a good deal."

"You got it," Steve called after him.

"Hey, thanks, Mr. Danger! You're a good guy!" And with that, Tony roared off down the driveway and out on to the street below.

"It's *Derringer*," Kelly shouted after the cab. "Why can't they ever get it straight?"

Steve just pulled her into his arms, hugging her tightly against him.

"Lady, you can't leave until I ask you a few questions. Am I making myself clear?"

"Perfectly." She couldn't stop smiling.

"Will you marry me?"

"But we're married."

"No, we're not."

"Yes, we are."

"Kel, follow my logic." And in front of God and the neighbors, and clad only in a bath towel, Steve Delany, famous actor and former master cynic, got down on one knee and began to propose.

"Steve, get up—"

"I can't live without you, Kelly. I don't want to. And I'm not getting up until you say yes. Marry me, and you'll make me a happy man."

"Yes, but—there's a man in the bushes!"

The camera clicked, and instantly the photographer launched himself into the small, unobtrusive blue Volvo parked down the tree-lined street. Both Steve and Kelly started to laugh as he swung her up into his arms and headed into the house.

"You've gotten me in more trouble than any woman I've ever known. And in the shortest amount of time. That should count for something."

"And just think... We've got the rest of our lives ahead of us."

"The world isn't ready." He kissed the tip of her nose, then smiled at her. "It's Mr. and Mrs. Derringer from now on."

"Mmmm. I like the sound of that."

He liked the way she rebounded so quickly. Once any danger was over, she was back to her sunny self. And Steve knew any black moods that might threaten to overcome him would have to deal with Kelly's relentless optimism.

It was a comforting thought.

"Well, Mrs. Derringer," he said, starting up the stairs, "how would you like to spend the rest of the day?"

"Do I get a choice?"

"Not if I can help it."

Much later, lying in bed, she trailed her fingers through the thicket of dark hair on his chest.

"Would you have come after me?"

"Oh, yeah."

Smiling, she snuggled closer against him.

They'd almost drifted off to sleep when she lifted her head, then raised herself up on one elbow.

"How come we never get around to being responsible?"

He curled his body more closely around her, enfolding her in his arms. "Maybe I like the idea of a dangerous little Derringer running around the house."

She caught her breath as she looked up at him.

"Really?"

"Yeah, really. You know, one of those babies of convenience."

"A classic plot device. And we could name him Nick—but only if it's a boy."

"Over my dead body."

The sound of her laughter filled the spacious bedroom, and Steve knew, with utter certainty, that in giving Kelly her miracle, he'd created another for himself.

She leaned up on her elbow again. "Are there any of those gun names left? How about Ruger Bearcat? Or Mauser? Wait, wait! If we have twins, we can name them Smith and Wesson—"

Laughing, he pulled her into his arms.

ROMANCE IS A YEARLONG EVENT!

Celebrate the most romantic day of the year with MY VALENTINE! (February)

CRYSTAL CREEK
When you come for a visit Texas-style, you won't want to leave! (March)

Celebrate the joy, excitement and adjustment that comes with being JUST MARRIED! (April)

Go back in time and discover the West as it was meant to be . . . UNTAMED— Maverick Hearts! (July)

LINGERING SHADOWS
New York Times bestselling author Penny Jordan brings you her latest blockbuster. Don't miss it! (August)

BACK BY POPULAR DEMAND!!!
Calloway Corners, involving stories of four sisters coping with family, business and romance! (September)

FRIENDS, FAMILIES, LOVERS
Join us for these heartwarming love stories that evoke memories of family and friends. (October)

Capture the magic and romance of Christmas past with HARLEQUIN HISTORICAL CHRISTMAS STORIES! (November)

WATCH FOR FURTHER DETAILS IN ALL HARLEQUIN BOOKS!

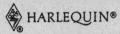

1993

The most romantic day of the year is here! Escape into the exquisite world of love with MY VALENTINE 1993. What better way to celebrate Valentine's Day than with this very romantic, sensuous collection of four original short stories, written by some of Harlequin's most popular authors.

ANNE STUART
JUDITH ARNOLD
ANNE McALLISTER
LINDA RANDALL WISDOM

THIS VALENTINE'S DAY, DISCOVER ROMANCE
WITH MY VALENTINE 1993

Available in February wherever Harlequin Books are sold.   VAL93

Take 4 bestselling love stories FREE
Plus get a FREE surprise gift!

COME FOR A VISIT—TEXAS-STYLE!

Where do you find hot Texas nights, smooth Texas charm and dangerously sexy cowboys? CRYSTAL CREEK!

This March, join us for a year in Crystal Creek...where power and influence live in the land, and in the hands of one family determined to nourish old Texas fortunes and to forge new Texas futures.

CRYSTAL CREEK reverberates with the exciting rhythm of Texas. Each story features the rugged individuals who live and love in the Lone Star State. And each one ends with the same invitation...

Y'ALL COME BACK...REAL SOON!

Watch for this exciting saga of a unique Texas family in March, wherever Harlequin Books are sold.

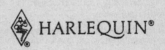

WELCOME TO

The quintessential small town, where everyone knows everybody else!

Each book set in Tyler is a self-contained love story; together, the twelve novels stitch the fabric of the community.

"The small town warmth and friendliness shine through."
Rendezvous

Join your friends in Tyler for the twelfth book, LOVEKNOT by Marisa Carroll, available in February.

Does Alyssa Baron really hold the key to Margaret's death? Will Alyssa and Edward consummate the romance they began more than thirty years ago?

GREAT READING...GREAT SAVINGS...AND A FABULOUS FREE GIFT!

With Tyler you can receive a fabulous gift, ABSOLUTELY FREE, by collecting proofs-of-purchase found in each Tyler book. And use our special Tyler coupons to save on your next TYLER book purchase.
